MURDER IN THE SQUARE:

A HITCHIN AFFAIR

BY JACOB AMOS

Advanced Review by:

Fake Lab CEO Gerald Dunstew

"Phwoar!"

For Bitchin' Hitchin!

ENDORSMENTS

"I couldn't put it down!"
Henry Bostick – Glue Hill, North Dorset

"Will have all men reaching for that cushion!"
Casper Couchstuffer – Shingay Cum Wendy, Cambs

"Finished off in one night. The end came too soon. Belter!"
Jock Hardcastle – Mount Pleasant, Avon

"Hilarious! It left my gums wetter than an otter's pocket!"
Phil McGrowler – Lower Swell, Cotswolds

"I'd give my right arm to write this good!"
Horatia Nelson – 52.8303* N, 0.8546* E, Norfolk

"Steamier than a sauna filled with boiling kettles!"
Herda Loudstrain – Crapstone, Devon

"I've got raw fingers from all the flicking. It's a page turner!"
Barbara Swallows – Dicks Mount, Suffolk

"It had our balloon knots in stitches down in the barracks!"
Private Rusti Sharrifs Baj, Nork Rise, Surrey

"When you think it's done, it sucks you back in!"
Jonny Hoover – Wetwang, Yorks

"Keep a defibrillator handy because I had a stroke!"
Desmond Thrutcher – Ramsbottom, Lancs

"../-/.--./.-./././...-././-../.-/.-../.-../---/-.--/-.../../..-/-/-/---/-./..."
Sammy Morse – Upper Chute, Hants

FOREWORD

First and foremost, this is a work of fiction. While reference may be made to actual events or existing locations, the names, characters, places, and incidents are either the product of the author's imagination or are used fictitiously. Any resemblance to any actual persons, living or dead, business establishments, events, or locales is entirely coincidental.
Any businesses that are real and mentioned are with the permission of the said business and are in no way linked to any real-life activity mentioned in this book, they are purely for explaining locations. All events mentioned in this book that take place in the town of Hitchin are entirely the work of fiction.

The actual town of Hitchin is based in Hertfordshire. It is a beautiful town with many wonderful shops and residents and is constantly featured various lists for top places to live in the U.K… so come and pay it a visit!

You will also notice that the chapters are set out in a (mostly!) sequential order of months so that following the timeline of events is kept simple and to the point.

I hope you enjoy reading it as much as I had fun writing it!

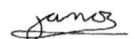

Chapters

Page 5 – November part 1: Let the Questions Begin!

Page 11 – January: On the Slopes & Dinner Gropes

Page 23 – February: Valentine Meals & Blood Spills

Page 35 – March: Rampant Easter Rabbits

Page 52 – April: A Shower of Fools

Page 62 – May: Picture Displays & Come What May

Page 72 – June: Long Days and Nights Can Be Murder

Page 82 – July: Don't Leave Me High

Page 96 – August: It Helps to Have a Dog

Page 112 – September: The More the Merrier

Page 122 – October: Trick and Most Definitely a Treat

Page 139 – November part 2: There Are No Saints

Page 149 – December: Jingle All You Slay

Page 168 – One Year Later: Life Blows On

November Part One:
Let the Questions Begin!

"Male, white, about 6 feet 4 inches tall, fair brown hair but receding on top. No distinguishing marks or tattoos" Inspector Matthews says to his partner. "All noted" Sergeant Carter responds. "It looks like that he was hit over the head with a blunt weapon. Weapon currently unknown. His head shows signs of trauma from the blow" Matthews continues.
"It looks like he might have been mugged too" replies Carter. "His pockets look like they've been turned out, maybe?" she concludes. "Hmm, maybe…" comes his reply.

The two detectives look down at the body for a moment longer before turning their attention to the rest of the police who are taping up the area. There are several squad cars parked across the High Street, with their blue lights on. The body of the man was only discovered thirty minutes ago by one of the town's residents who was on an early morning jog through the market square, and only because it was light enough to see the pool of blood on the floor beside them, otherwise they might have easily been mistaken for someone who had been so drunk that they could have fallen into the pile of black sacks of rubbish that were piled up for collection by the lone shed that sits on the edge of the square.

Matthews looks around at his surroundings, noticing the time on the blue clock in the middle of the square, 6:45am. Matthews and Carter then proceed to take a slow walk around the square, looking for clues that may help them.
"Sir, we've found a wallet" remarks PC Ellary.
Matthews dons a pair of gloves and takes the wallet from the PC and opens it up to see that it's empty apart from a debit card with the deceased name on it.
After passing it to Carter he pulls out an evidence bag as Carter places the wallet inside. "Take this to forensics would you please?" he instructs the PC.

Matthews looks back again at Carter and says, "I think it's time that we had a little chat to his friends". Carter looks up at him puzzled and asks, "What makes you think this is the click?". Matthews looks back down at the body and replies, "This might look like a random mugging, but something tells me that it isn't, more like a cover up". Carter looks at him then pulls out her notebook. "Who shall we pay a visit to first?". Matthews looks at her and replies, "Take your pick at this rate".
Inspector Matthews clearly recognises the recently deceased victim, having crossed paths several times this year, notably from local functions and from him being a high-profile resident of the town.

"Coffee sir?" asks Cater, observing that one of the town centre coffee shops lights have come on and a staff member unlocking the doors. "Yes, please Carter, americano, no sugar, soy milk if possible" he replies with a smile, clearly still tired from being woken up so early on his day off. As Carter heads off to the coffee shop, Matthews takes a short walk into Churchyard, then Churchgate, then across to the entrance to Sun Street and then Bucklersbury, looking for any other possible clues. Whilst he does this more and more people come out from their flats above the shops, wondering what is going on. One lady from Coopers Yard kindly brings a flask of tea out and some cups for some of the officers on the scene.

After a few minutes Carter comes back out and hands a cup of coffee to Matthews, who thanks her. After a few sips Matthews looks up and around the high posts to spot where the CCTV cameras are located. "PC Sale?" shouts Matthews. "Yes sir?" comes her reply. "Sale, can you obtain the CCTV footage please from the market square camera? But could you also get the footage from all other CCTV cameras within a five-hundred-meter radius too?".

"Right away sir" she replies as she departs. "What is it?" Carter asks Matthews. "A hunch. Something doesn't sit right with me on this one" he replies to her, with a knowing look in his eyes. They walk back to their cars and depart for the local station to continue their investigation.

A couple of days later Carter receives a call from the Pathology department from the local hospital. She takes some notes and heads over to inspector Mathew's desk. "Sir, we've got the details back about the body" she tells him. "He was killed around midnight, could be earlier, could be after". Matthews looks at Carter as she continues, "A Halloween mugging gone wrong?". Matthews ponders her question then replies that he doesn't think so. "Another thing, he had traces of alcohol, cocaine and cannabis too" she concludes. "Yep, I'm not surprised by that one" he counters, before announcing to Carter, "OK, let's pay them all another visit". Carter nods her head in agreement and asks, "Who first?". He goes through his notes and replies, "Start with Josh, he's a good guy".
Later that day, Matthews and Carter make their way over to pay a visit to Josh. "Hi Josh, may we come in?" Carter asks him. "Yeah sure, come on in, everything OK?" he asks them. "Let's talk inside" replies Matthews.

Josh is a national events manager, being part of some of the U. K's most high profile sporting events.
Judith is an area manager for a high-profile chain of health centre's that dominate the U.K.

As they enter, Judith comes down the stairs to be greeted by the police again, not for the first time this year. "Hello officers!" she greets them, looking surprised. "Hi Judith, how are you?" asks Carter with a warm smile. "Not too bad thanks, how's the family?" she replies. "Getting bigger by the day!" Carter replies.
Matthews interjects, "Sorry this isn't a happy visit". Josh and Judith look at the two officers as their smiles disappear and their expressions become more serious.

Josh, clearly sensing that something is wrong asks, "What's happened? I've seen that look on you before". Carter replies, "There's been another murder" as Matthews goes on to tell them who has been murdered. Josh and Judith look horrified, a little bit in disbelief but also not overly surprised.

"How many is that now?" Josh asks. Matthews replies, "That makes four now from those that you know".

"Shit!" exclaims Judith, looking at Josh, now quite worried. Josh puts his arm around her to reassure her. Carter looks at them both a little sympathetic then tells them, "I'm sorry we come bearing bad news again, but, as protocol we must ask you where you were on the night of the 31st of October". Judith replies, "We were at a Halloween party over at John and Lynda's house". Matthews replies, "Can you tell us what time from and to?". Josh replies, "Yes of course, we got there about 8pm and didn't leave until about 1am in the morning, when our taxi picked us up". Matthews nods to appreciate the honest responses as Carter makes notes on her pad.

The four of them take a seat in the living room and go through what details are allowed to be discussed.

"Thanks for your time both of you" Matthews tells them, as he and Carter make their way outside.

"Who's next? John and Lynda?" Carter asks. Matthews nods to agree as they both get back in the car and make their way to the next couple.

The two officers arrive at Knights Road at John and Lynda's home. This is one of the most prestigious roads to live on. It is where the wealthiest residents reside, where they rub shoulders with high profile neighbours from all types of backgrounds. Bankers, sports stars, T.V and film celebrities, music stars, professionals from various jobs who are at the top of their tree, business owners, investors and more.

John is a high-profile lawyer, who regularly attends the high court in London. His wide Lynda is a high-profile actress, famous for roles on T.V and several British films.

Matthews and Carter knock on their door and as they greet each other, the officers go inside to tell them the news. John is shocked to hear about the latest death, and more to the point that they know the person well.
"As you'll appreciate, we must ask where you were last night" Carter tells them. Lynda leads them to the function room to show them. "We were right here, we held our annual Halloween party" Lynda remarks, gesturing to the officers to look around at the mess.
John butts in to apologise about the mess as they haven't had time to clear up. "It's no issue to me, I appreciate you are both very busy people" Carter replies.

"Can you tell me who else was at the party?" asks Carter to Lynda. Lynda thinks as she recalls and replies, "Sure, there was Josh and Judith, Tom, Tyler, Steve, Kirsty, Andrew, Kate, Geoff and Claire". Matthews looks at her and asks, "No Harry or Clio then? Were they not invited?". John jumps in with, "They were but they never showed up". Matthews looks puzzled as he concludes with, "Harry I can understand, but Clio? That is a bit of a surprise". By now Carter can see the cogs in Matthews's head turning as he weighs up the information given to him.

As they are about to exit the room Matthews stops and turns to John and Lynda and says, "By the time we are gone, I am going to assume of course that the coffee table will be nice and clean?". Carter glances over to see a pile of vapes, empty glasses, smoked joint ends and dusty white powder with various small transparent bags littered around it, including several fifty-pound notes rolled tightly. John and Lynda look at each other sheepishly before turning to look back at the officers. John stutters "Yes, yes of course!" before hurrying over to the offending table to make an instant start on cleaning it up.
Lynda looks down at the floor and manages to mumble an apology, to which Matthews raises an eyebrow and walks out of the house with Carter.
"Sir, I don't understand, if we searched the house we may have found more" she asks him.

Matthews stops and turns to tell her, "Right now we have bigger things to deal with, but I think a warning to them has been sent" as his face softens with a wry smile. Carter nods to agree and smiles, as they head back to the car. "Who's next?" Carter asks him. "Let's pay a visit to the other party guests then after them we will pay Clio a little visit". Carter looks at him with some concern on her face as she asks him, "Don't you think she will be quite upset still?". Matthews keeps walking along the road as he replies with, "Depends on how upset she actually is". Carter opens the gate to the next house as she replies, "I hope you know what you are doing!" as Matthews just smiles and rings the doorbell.
Throughout the day, Inspector Matthews and Sergeant Carter pay a visit to all the party guests that John and Lynda listed for them.
This includes:

Tom and Tyler – They own a string of popular eateries in Hitchin.

Steve and Kirsty – He is a business investor who live off the profits. She doesn't work and goes to the local gym on most days.

Andrew and Katie – They are media company directors. They also like to openly indulge in hedonistic lifestyles with other people in their open relationship.

Geoff and Claire – He owns a budding pharmaceutical company, and she works for the government as a junior minister.

The last port of call is to Clio. They knock on the door but no answer. Matthews tries to look through a front window. Just then, Carter's phone rings as she paces away to answer it, as Matthews tries once more to get a response at the front door. "Sir, we have the CCTV footage back, and you're not going to believe this!" she tells him.

January:
On the Slopes & Dinner Gropes

"HAPPY BIRTHDAY" they all shout out. Josh has a broad smile as they pop corks of several bottles of champagne. "Happy birthday darling!" Judith says to him, handing him a gift. He gives Judith a kiss and thanks her, then thanks everyone else too, as they pass him a glass of bubbles. "Here you go buddy" says Andrew, passing his gift to Josh, as do the others in turn. "Thank you everyone, it is much appreciated!" he tells them.

The friends have gone away skiing for a few days to the Swiss Alps to celebrate Josh's birthday. They have gone to the chalet that is owned by Geoff and Claire at Les Crosets, Switzerland.
The friends that have made the trip includes:

Josh & Judith, Geoff & Claire, Andrew & Katie, Steve & Kirsty, Tom & Tyler, Dominic & Nicole.

Dominic is a clinical director at the local hospital for his department. Nicole, his wife, is the owner of the towns biggest botox clinic, with a client list of well-known public figures.

Josh excitedly opens his presents from each couple. He receives a top of the range sports watch from his wife Judith. Geoff and Claire give him a new orange ski jacket, Andrew and Katie have bought him a weekend stay at a top London hotel, Steve and Kirsty give him a very old and expensive bottle of his favourite whisky, Tom and Tyler bought him a top of the range sat-nav bike computer, and Dominic and his wife Nicole give him a series of clinic vouchers from her business, plus all-expense paid vouchers to his favourite places to go in Hitchin, including the Hermitage Road Restaurant, and for Wisbey Osteopathy on Bancroft, where Sam helps to keep him fighting fit as Josh is keen on the various sports he enjoys.

"Ok enough of all that gushy stuff!" Katie announces to the gathered friends, "Let's get the party started!", at which point she proceeds to pull out a rather large looking bag of what could only be cocaine. "How the hell did you manage to find and get that?!" exclaims Steve, as the others burst out laughing. "We have friends back in the UK who are friends with a Swiss couple, and they kindly delivered to us yesterday whilst you lot were out skiing" Andrew replies with a wink and a smile. Claire then asks Katie and Andrew with a wink, "Regular friends or your partner swapping friends?". Andrew and Katie laugh and reply in unison, "Swapping friends!". Kirsty remarks to Katie, "No wonder you guys didn't want to come skiing yesterday!" to which Katie giggles, then replies, "I did, but not skiing!". Nicole bursts out laughing and calls Katie a filthy cow. It is said in jest, as friends who are close can throw affectionate insults at each other. Dominic looks at Andrew and with a chuckle, asks him, "I hope we're not sitting anywhere that naked bottoms have been?!". Andrew laughs and reassures his friends that they used their own bedroom. "Thank God we have a cleaner!" remarks Claire, as all the friends laugh.

The party is now in full swing as the friends put on a party play list of music, turn on the disco lights, pour each other more drinks as more corks fly out from bottles of champagne, and the rather large bag of cocaine is tipped onto the glass coffee table for them all to indulge in.

The next day, all the friends take to the slopes once the entrance to the gondolas is opened. Each gondola only holds four people at a time, so when they all line up to enter one, Tom quickly steps forward to the one that Josh, Judith, and Geoff are entering.
As they quickly settle inside the gondola, Tom speaks to Josh, "Mate, I wanted to ask you a question and I know that this trip was for your birthday, but I didn't want to be a thunder stealer".

Josh looks at his friend puzzled but smiles and says, "Of course mate what is it?". At which point Tom pulls out a small box, that he opens to reveal and a platinum ring. Judith instantly squeals with delight as she asks Tom, "Are you going to propose to Tyler?", to which Tom smiles broadly and nods. Josh and Geoff instantly hug their friend and tell him that they couldn't think of a more beautiful place to do so, on top of snow-capped mountains surrounded by their best friends. This makes Tom very happy as he carefully puts the ring away.

As the friends reach the top of the gondola lift and regroup, they head off down the first slope. After about an hour of skiing, they stop for a quick coffee at one of the many cafes and bars that adorn the area. The scene is perfect, with snow covered mountain peaks reflecting the rays of the sun on a clear blue-sky day.
Judith pops the cork off a bottle of champagne as she begins to fill up twelve glasses. Tyler looks puzzled as the other friends pretend to ignore him, so he asks Claire, "Champagne so early? What's the occasion?", but before she can reply, Tom says to him, "Yours!". Tyler turns around to see Tom down on one knee with the ring in his hand. "You are my best friend, my confident, my rock, will you marry me, Tyler?". The friends all hold their breath as Tyler holds his hands up to his face and gasps, his eyes wide open. Tyler instantly drops to his knees and throws his arms around Tom and shouts, "Of course I will!" as the two of them hug tightly. The friends all cheer and begin to pass glass of bubbles around to each other in celebration. Other skiers who witnessed the occasion come over to congratulate the happy couple.
Meanwhile, back in Hitchin, Harry and Clio are hosting a dinner party for their friends. The dinner party is to welcome their new neighbours who have just moved in next door to them, on the much sought-after Knights Road.

Harry is a property investor. He buys and sells land and buildings then breaks them into smaller land plots to sell on for higher profit. He has reached a point in his life that he has bought and sold enough to live off the profits from his acquired fortune. Harry is a man's man but with an air of arrogance and swagger, an alpha male type.
His wife Clio is a glamourous lady, strong-willed, an alpha female if you like, who doesn't need to work due to her husband's amassed fortune. Instead, she spends her days keeping fit, heading to the local gym to take part in classes and drink coffee afterwards with the other ladies that she has built up friendships with, not to mention a great opportunity to listen to and deliver their own gossip on what is going on in their lives, but mostly about other peoples.

Harry stands up at the head of the dinner table and announces to the gathered friends, "I'd like to propose a toast to welcome our new neighbours to our wonderful town". All the guests raise their glasses and call out brokenly, "Welcome James and Elizabeth".
James stands up and directs his attention to Harry but addressing the guests, "Thank you Harry and Clio for putting on this wonderful dinner and thank you everyone for welcoming us to the area" as he raises his glass in thanks. Harry and James sit back down as everyone continues their conversations.
"So, James, how long have you been a man of the cloth?" asks John. James replies with, "Oh, let me think, about two years now". Lynda follows up with, "So where did you live before this?". Elizabeth, James's wife, looks at her husband as he replies, "We were based in Hampshire, but I go where God sends me!" to which Lynda smiles and replies, "Yes, of course".
John and Lynda of course, you have already met before. As for the other guests present, there is:

Enrique, Indya, Sebastian, Rebecca, Phil, and Maddie.

Enrique is a seasoned professional footballer who plays for a well-established premier league team based in London. He is very famous in the town and had a lot of adoring fans. His is also very good looking with quite a large female fanbase. His wife Indya, used to be a model but gave it up after giving birth to their two small children. She leads a very comfortable lifestyle and is the envy of many women of the town.

Sebastian is an app and webpage designer for high profile clients and businesses. He works mostly from home and lives next door to the new arrivals that are James and Elizabeth, the other side to Harry and Clio. His wife Rebecca is a GP at her local practice in Hitchin. On the side she also consults and delivers medical training at hospitals and clinics.

Phil is the CEO of a national building company, having worked his way up through the ranks from starting on the tools to the position he is in today. Maddie, his wife, is an investment banker who works in the city for a global company.

Indya asks Elizabeth, "So how did you and the Reverend James meet?". Elizabeth looks at her with a glint in her eye and replies, "Oh we met at a club quite a while ago, he wasn't always a man of God!" at which point the Reverend James coughs loud enough to interrupt the rest of the story. Indya chuckles, as does Rebecca.
"Forgive me for asking, to move to such a beautiful home, does the church pay well?" Rebecca asks James. Before he can reply Elizabeth says with a half-smile, "What makes you think it's his money".
Rebecca blushes slightly and apologies to Elizabeth. "Nonsense!" she replies. "Don't be sorry, the truth is that his parents died some time ago. They were extremely wealthy, and James is an only child" Elizabeth concludes, flashing a smile at Rebecca, showing her confidence in her surroundings. Rebecca smiles back politely and turns her attentions elsewhere.

Elizabeth turns to Clio and asks her, "Would you kindly tell me which way to the bathroom please?". Before Clio has a chance to answer Enrique answers for her, "I'm in need myself, but you can go before me, let me show you". Elizabeth thanks him as she is about to get up. "Allow me" he tells her, putting his hands on the back of her chair to pull it back as she is about to get up. Enrique looks down at her legs in admiration, then, as she shuffles to stand up, he notices the tops of her stockings, just showing, as she wriggles her skirt down enough to hide them from the other guests seeing. She stands up and thanks Enrique for being a gentleman, but gives him a suggestive look, as her eyes look down at his waist, noticing that what he saw had aroused him. Instead of trying to conceal or feel embarrassed, he simply smiles back at her as he pushes her chair under the table.

The other guests continue to talk amongst themselves as Enrique and Elizabeth walk down the hallway. "I must say, James is a very lucky man to have found such a beautiful lady like you" he tells her. She looks at him with a knowing smile and thanks him. As they reach the bathroom door, she stops and turns to Enrique, then steps close to him and whispers, "I noticed that what I am wearing you quite liked". Enrique smiles broadly and replies matter-of-factly, "When you have it, flaunt it". She looks him dead in the eyes and replies, "Oh, I do!", as she opens the door to the bathroom and walks in, closing the door slowly, slow enough to look back at him smiling, a glint in her suggestive eyes. As the door closes Enrique smiles to himself, then checks his looks in the mirror in the hallway.

After a couple of minutes Elizabeth exits the bathroom, seeing that Enrique has waited patiently for his turn, she smiles at him.
As she makes her way back down the hallway, she turns back to see him watching her. She stops and urns to him. "Do you know that club just out of town?" she asks him. "You mean Santorini's?" he replies.

"That's the one. I like it there" she says, before continuing, "My husband works away a lot with his job. I don't know many people here. I'll be there Saturday night hoping to make some new friends". Enrique looks at her and replies, "It's my favourite place to unwind after home games" as he gives her a suggestive look, letting her read between the lines. She smiles at him and turns to walk away again, pausing once more to look back and finish with, "It's always nice to meet new friends". Enrique grins at her, taking on board what she said and the way that she delivered it, then subtly he eyes her up and down before replying, "I'll be there". She smiles at him then winks, as she disappears back to the dining area.

Back in Switzerland at the chalet, the friends all enjoy dinner together as they drink and chat amongst themselves. The wives are at one end of the table and the men at the other. Judith, Claire, Katie, Kirsty, and Nicole discuss their lives before Katie delivers some gossip.
"Ladies, have you heard a rumour about Maddie?".
Kirsty pipes up quickly with, "Ooh, no? What is it?". Katie leans in and lowers her tone as she continues, "I've heard a rumour, and it's just a rumour remember, that Maddie might be playing away from home, if you know what I mean!".
Judith and Claire giggle as they ask Katie who it might be, but Katie shrugs her shoulders to suggest she genuinely doesn't know.
Kirsty asks Katie how she heard this information. "Just whispers through my usual circle of late-night friends!" she tells her.
Nicole speaks up to tell the ladies, "Come on, it's just whispers, she's our friend, it's not fair on her, besides, if anything was then I'm sure one of us would know by now".
Kirsty replies to Nicole with, "You're very good friends with her, surely you must know something?!".
Nicole looks back at her unimpressed and counters, "Even if I did, I wouldn't be gossiping about it".

Kirsty looks back at Nicole for a moment longer than usual to see if she thinks she is telling the truth, then smiles and turns away to eavesdrop on what the men are talking about.

Back in Hitchin, the dinner party concludes as the guests begin to depart. Harry and Clio say their goodbyes to them all as they start to exit the doorway. Clio gives the reverend a hug and kisses him on the cheek and repeats her greeting of welcoming him and Elizabeth to the area. At the same time, Harry gives Elizabeth a hug telling her it was lovely to meet her, but as he does, her hand slips lower down and rests gently on his bottom, not enough to suggest a squeeze, but enough to make a statement. Harry gently pulls away from her, smiling back at her as she looks deep into his eyes and thanks him for a lovely evening and that she looks forward to coming over again soon. As they close the door Clio turns to Harry and says, "I think that went quite well. They seem like a nice couple" to which Harry replies that they are. "She's quite beautiful, isn't she?" Clio asks him. Harry looks at Clio and brushes the comment off with, "She's OK". Clio scoffs at his comment and replies, "No need to lie Harry! You know she is". Harry smiles back and doesn't say thing as he begins to remove his cufflinks on his shirt. Clio steps forward to get close to Harry as she moves her hand towards then down his trousers, then remarks, "Early night?". Harry chuckles as he lets her continue what she is doing as they turn to head upstairs. As they climb the stairs, Clio makes sure that Harry can see her stocking tops peeking under the hemline of her dress. She stops momentarily to turn and declare to him, "Just remember who the real Queen of the Knight is", letting her play on word sentence sink in as Harry smirks.

Back in Hitchin, the dinner party concludes as the guests begin to depart. Harry and Clio say their goodbyes to them all as they start to exit the doorway.

Clio gives the reverend a hug and kisses him on the cheek and repeats her greeting of welcoming him and Elizabeth to the area.
At the same time, Harry gives Elizabeth a hug telling her it was lovely to meet her, but as he does, her hand slips lower down and rests gently on his bottom, not enough to suggest a squeeze, but enough to make a statement.
Harry gently pulls away from her, smiling back at her as she looks deep into his eyes and thanks him for a lovely evening and that she looks forward to coming over again soon. As they close the door Clio turns to Harry and says, "I think that went quite well. They seem like a nice couple" to which Harry replies that they are. "She's quite beautiful, isn't she?" Clio asks him. Harry looks at Clio and brushes the comment off with, "She's OK". Clio scoffs at his comment, "No need to lie Harry! You know she is". Harry smiles but doesn't say anything as he removes the cufflinks on his shirt. Clio moves forward and puts her hand down his trousers, then remarks, "Early night?". Harry chuckles as he lets her continue what she is doing as they turn to head upstairs. As they climb the stairs, Clio makes sure that Harry can see her stocking tops peeking under the hemline of her dress. She stops momentarily to turn and declare to him, "Just remember who the real Queen of the Knight is", letting her play on words sink into the smirking Harry. The problem now though is that his thoughts are elsewhere.

Saturday arrives and Enrique has just finished his match. He messages Indya to tell her that he is going into town with some of the other footballers to celebrate their win. She replies to him to not wake her when he gets home.
Instead, Enrique drives direct to Santorini's.
He enters and immediately scans the club. His eyes quickly fix on lady at the bar. As he walks towards her his eyes look her up and down.

She is wearing black lace up stilettos and a black high neck backless figure-hugging dress, complete with a gold necklace and clutch bag. Her hair is dark brown with added curls at the bottom, she has hazel eyes and subtle red lipstick. "Hello Elizabeth!" he says, grinning like a Cheshire cat. She picks up her drink and takes a sip as she looks at him seductively and replies, "I was hoping you would come". Enrique eyes her up and down and compliments her in her outfit to which she thanks him. "Would you like to sit down somewhere a little more private so we can enjoy each other's company?" he asks her. She responds with a smile and stands up, as Enrique takes hold of her drink as they walk to the VIP booths. The VIP area is a very exclusive area, which has its own booths that are shieled away from prying eyes, complete with leather sofas and swanky tables and plants, with frosted glass doors for privacy. The perfect place to be out in public yet not be seen by anyone.

They sit down on the large sofa together as they make small talk. As she is telling him about how they are settling in nicely in their new home, Enrique puts his hand on her thigh and begins to gently stroke her leg. She glances down at his hand and a smile comes over her face, clearly enjoying what he is doing. He takes his hand away, wondering if he has misread the situation. She leans over to whisper in his ear, "Did I ask you to stop?". Enrique grins and continues to stroke her leg again. Elizabeth uncrosses her legs and lies back into the sofa, drink in hand, looking at him with a knowing look in her eyes. Enrique leans forward to kiss her, but she puts her finger to his lips and tells him, "I'd prefer your lips to be kissing me elsewhere first". He sits up, smiles broadly, puts his drink down and stands up. Elizabeth looks up at him lustily. Enrique smiles then drops down to his knees as she begins to part her knees to make room for him.

One week later, the ski friends have arrived back in the UK and have returned quickly to their routines of work and life.

Josh, ever the social bug that he is, sends a message in the men's WhatsApp group to ask if anyone would like to go for a drink on Saturday.
His phone pings back with replies from Sebastian, Geoff, Steve, and Phil that they are going to come along. Harry messages to say that he is away on business for a couple of weeks but will join them on another one when he gets back.

Saturday arrives and the men make their way to the Lytton Arms in Knebworth for drinks. After a couple of beers each and much catching up, Josh asks them if they fancy going to Santorini's, to which they agree.
Upon arrival the friends head to the bar area and pull up a stool and begin to talk about their week.
As Sebastian listens to their tales, he glances around to see Enrique walking across, accompanied by a woman, towards the VIP booths.
Sebastian watches him, wondering who he is with. It is clearly not his wife.
He gets up and follows him as far as the bouncers will let him go. He is about to call out to Enrique but quickly stops as he suddenly realises it is Elizabeth. Sebastian's mouth opens in astonishment, quickly replaced by a grin.
He takes his phone out and takes a picture, thinking to himself that it might come in handy in the future.
Knowledge, after all, is power.
"Where did you go?" Josh asks him quizzically. "I saw an old school mate, just saying hello to him" comes Sebastian's reply, as Josh gives him a thumbs up.
Sebastian smiles at him and sips his drink, rejoining the conversations taking place amongst his friends, but glancing across to the VIP booths once more, his mouth making a wry smile.

Later that evening, as the men party with the other club's guests, Enrique and Elizabeth emerge from the booth.
As they do, a guest from another booth spots Enrique and goes over to him to talk to him, but it quickly escalates into a shoving match.

The guest grabs Enrique by the throat and is shouting in his face. Sebastian spots this as he has been looking over frequently.
He gets up and takes his phone out to film the scene unfolding. The guest pushes Enrique backwards and lunges forward menacingly, but as he does the bouncers quickly intervene to restrain him, the guest though is undeterred and tried to fight them off, throwing a punch that lands in the face of a bouncer. The other bouncers react quickly and wrestle the man to the floor.
Elizabeth in incensed by the guest and screams at him as Enrique watches on, almost laughing at the guest.
The guest shouts something at Elizabeth, something that must have been quite an insult, as she suddenly swings her leg back and kicks the guest as hard as she can in the head. Sebastian is shocked by this, his phone in his hand, filming it all. By now, some other guests in the club have turned their attention to the VIP booth area, wondering what is going on, as other club staff members have by now rushed over to help escort Enrique and Elizabeth out of the club via the back entrance. The other guests are unaware that it is them as their faces are shielded by the staff, but it is too late, as Sebastian has witnessed it all.

It is 2am, as the friends leave the club and get a taxi back to Hitchin. Everyone is quite drunk as they talk rubbish to each other, laughing at their own jokes and making the taxi drivers life harder than it should be. Sebastian though, is deep in thought, as he thinks about what to do, what his next move will be, what to do with the information he has gathered from seeing Enrique and Elizabeth. Once he is home, he reviews the pictures that he took and the video that he shot of Enrique and Elizabeth, as a smile appears on his face, the cogs in his head turning about what he is thinking about doing next.

"How was your night?" Rebecca asks him. "Very good, better than expected" comes his reply, smiling to himself, as he gets undressed and climbs into bed with his wife.

February:
Valentine Meals & Blood Spills

Early February, it is raining as the people of Hitchin go about their daily lives as the town is a sea of umbrellas and of people seeking refuge in the coffee shops and eateries. Inside the Nook coffee shop, Elizabeth sits, drinking coffee, busy texting on her phone. Steve is walking by and spots her, so he enters and greets her. She invites him to sit down and join her.
"How are you settling in?" he asks her. "Very well, thank you" she replies, but with a smile on her face that only she knows means better than expected. "That's good to hear" he responds, giving her a smile. "Have you made many friends yet?" he asks her. "Just a few, but it's always good to make more" she replies to him, sipping her coffee and looking directly at him. Steve smiles back as he looks outside to see that it is pouring down now.
She glances outside too, observing how much it is raining. As she does so, Steve looks back at her and pays a bit more attention to her, admiring her legs and black knee length boots. Elizabeth turns her face back just in time to see that he is looking at her, and too late for him to turn his attention back up to her face. She looks at him and smiles as she sips more coffee.
"Tell me, what do the people of this town do when it rains this hard? It's too miserable outside to enjoy everyday pursuits" she asks him, smiling. "I suppose people probably just stay inside and make their own fun" comes his reply.
Steve and Elizabeth sit there in silence as they smile at each other, as he thinks about what he has said and wondering what she is thinking.
Steve's phone suddenly rings so he takes the call, speaking to what must be a business-related call. As he does, Elizabeth removes her small black jacket to reveal a low-cut black dress that she is wearing.
As Steve continues to talk on his phone, he glances over to look at Elizabeth, as she sips her coffee, apparently browsing her phone, but her wry smile tells another story.

Steve smiles to himself as he ends the phone call and diverts his attention back to her. "Busy man" she tells him with a smile. Steve replies with, "Sometimes, but I do get quite a bit of time to myself during the day. I have an office at home to work remotely from but it's nicer to pop into town, besides, it's always nice to bump into people". Elizabeth looks at him, takes another sip of coffee before putting her cup down, she stands up and puts her jacket back on. Steve smiles as she does so, perhaps a little disappointed that she is leaving. As she is about to walk off, she stops and tells him, "Next time you are around and fancy a coffee, give me a call, it's always nice to have good company". Steve smiles broadly and gives her his number. He sends her a message on his to which she sees and saves his number.

"Give me a call sometime when you are free, don't be a stranger" he tells her. "She puts her phone away, looks at him and replies with a hint of suggestion, "I will", as she smiles and turns to walk away. Steve watches her walk out of the café and past the window. As she does, she looks through the window at him and smiles broadly, knowing that he is watching her leave. Steve smiles broadly to himself, having enjoyed the brief meeting, his mind wanders, thinking about her words. Two minutes later, Steve's phone pings. He reads the message from Elizabeth. "Coffee tomorrow at mine?".

Steve smiles to himself and simply replies, "Yes".

"See you at 10am X" comes her reply. This excites Steve, to the point where he uses his coat when standing up to conceal the obvious excitement.

The next morning, Sebastian is in his study, working on the latest app that he has been employed to do for a national company. As he glances outside, he sees Steve outside and walk down the path leading to the reverends and Elizabeth's house. He stands up to glance more at what he is up to.

He gets his phone out and takes a picture.

Not much to view really, but having witnessed the scenes in Santorini's recently, he suspects that anything is possible, even an innocent looking house call.
His curiosity has been piqued so he heads downstairs and out into his garden. He peers carefully over the fence that divides their gardens, using one of the trees for cover, to not be seen. As he focuses his eyes, he can see that Steve and Elizabeth are chatting and having coffee. As he continues to watch he notices that Elizabeth is dressed up, quite smart, sexily even, especially for someone who is just mulling around their own home. He continues to watch and then his eyes widen slightly as he watches them both put down their cups and leave the room, only to spot them both through a first-floor window walking up the stairs, then seeing them in what must be one of the house bedrooms. He secretly snaps a few more pictures, but then, the curtains close. Sebastian is smart enough to work out what must be going on, as it hardly seems like she is giving him a tour of the house and showing how wonderful her light bulbs look in the dark.

The next day a message pops up in the men's WhatsApp group. It is Phil, passing on some news. "Chaps! You know that night we went to Santorini's? Some bloke was beaten up and is in a critical condition in hospital!". Josh replies in the group, "Wow! How did we miss that?!". Phil replies, "I know! Apparently, he was taken to hospital and spent a couple of nights there, but the news says he was taken ill from his injuries, collapsed at home, and was taken back. Apparently, he's on at intensive care unit, with support to keep him alive!". "Christ!" Josh replies. As the two friends continue to trade texts, Sebastian replies with just emojis, but he knows what really happened, having witnessed Enrique and Elizabeth together, and now having seen Steve pay Elizabeth a home visit too.
He smiles to himself as he thinks about this news.
The other men in the group also reply, except Harry and Steve, something that Sebastian doesn't pick up currently.

Sebastian checks the time on his watch, seeing that it is early afternoon. He knows that Rebecca will not be home until the early evening, and he spots outside that the reverends car is not home. He thinks for a moment about what he has seen so far, convincing himself that Elizabeth must be quite liberal in her choice of social activities. He pours himself a quick whisky, downs it, then exits his home and knocks on his neighbour's door. "Oh, hello Sebastian, how are you?" she asks him, looking surprised that he has paid her a visit. He smiles at her and replies, "Fine thanks, I was just next door and wanted a break from working so I thought I would come and say hello and see if you wanted a coffee or something". She looks at him and smiles politely as she hesitates for a moment but then invites him in.

In the kitchen she makes him a coffee as they sit at the kitchen island. Sebastian looks at her as they make small talk about her time in the town so far. He then changes the subject to Santorini's. "How did you find Santorini's?" he asks her. She looks at him, surprised at his comment, knowing that he has asked her how she found it rather than had she been there yet. She looks at him as her smile falls slightly to one of a more deadpan look as she replies carefully, "I have popped my head in to take a look". Sebastian smiles at her as he replies with a coy smile, "Yes, I thought I saw you there recently". "Really?" comes her reply. Sebastian can now see that she is a little uncomfortable. Elizabeth thinking to herself on how she was spotted but didn't see him. "If you saw me then you should have come over to say hello" she replies, testing him, waiting to see what his reply will be. Unfortunately for her, it's not one that she wanted. Sebastian looks her right in the eyes and replies, "I would have, but you looked like you were already busy!". Elizabeth shuffles uncomfortably in her chair, caught for words, but then replies, "What do you mean?". Sebastian takes his phone out and shows her a picture of her with Enrique in the VIP section, looking quite cozy together. "I bumped into him in the club, and he invited me for a drink, he was just being friendly" she protests calmly. "Really?" comes his reply.

Sebastian then swipes across a couple of times to show her the picture of Steve next door with her, downstairs then upstairs. Elizabeth shuffles slightly in her seat and replies, "He just popped in to say hello, so I showed him a tour of the home, he was curious". Sebastian chuckles as he replies in a slightly sarcastic tone, "Did her enjoy the tour?". She smiles back at him and remains silent, trying not to say anything further that would fuel his intrigue. Sebastian pauses for a moment then swipes back to the video he took at the club and plays it to her in its entirety. By now Elizabeth is quite uncomfortable and visibly annoyed. "Why are you taking videos of me?" she demands. "I heard a commotion and started to film it, as people do! You can imagine my surprise when I saw you kick that man in the head!". Elizabeth does her best to hide her emotions, but inside she is angry, at Sebastian but also with herself for being seen, not wanting to let anything on or slip that Sebastian may now use against her. "Did you know that this man is now in a coma? On life support?". Elizabeth looks away from him, trying her best to keep a blank expression, then looks back at him and snaps, "If you saw the whole thing, you would have seen that the bouncers went in heavy handed with him!". Sebastian laughs and replies, "Hey! I'm not suggesting anything! I'm just showing you what I saw!". Elizabeth looks at him, trying to work out his intentions. She doesn't need to wait long though.

"You don't need to worry Elizabeth, no one else has seen it, we are friends after all. She looks at him blankly, then thinking about what he has said, she thanks him, not wholeheartedly, but enough to carry weight behind the meaning.

Sebastian though, follows up with, "Maybe we could be good friends".

She looks at him to work out his meaning behind his words.

He looks at her, smiling, leering almost. He then proceeds to look her up and down slowly, before putting his hand out to stroke her leg and declares, "Maybe we could be very good friends".

Elizabeth watches his hand, emotionless.
The look in her eyes suggests that this is not what she wants, but Sebastian isn't concerned about that. Just then, the front door opens, and the reverend comes into the kitchen, greeting them both, as he gives his wife a kiss on the cheek. They make brief small talk then Elizabeth declares she will see their guest out. As Sebastian leaves, he turns to Elizabeth and says, "I look forward to seeing you again very soon, perhaps next time maybe I can have a tour of the house..." leaving his words to linger. She looks at him sternly and replies, "Maybe". He chuckles at her as his parting words to her are, "You can trust me, I am good with secrets" referring to the pictures and video on his phone, as turns and walks away. She watches him leave and shuts the door. Her husband James walks over to her in the hallway and asks if everything is OK, seeing that she is not exactly in a happy mood. "I'm fine, just having an interesting conversation with our new neighbour" she replies. "How was your day?" she asks him. "Interesting also, I went back to Hampshire today to take care of some old business" he replies, as they both walk back into the kitchen to continue their conversation.

Valentines Day. Some of the couples are making their own plans to spend the day and evening in their own romantic ways. Josh and Judith have planned to go to the Hermitage Bar and Restaurant for a meal. Geoff and Claire have booked a table at one of the local restaurants that belong to Tom and Tyler. Phil and Maddie, along with Dominic and Nicole, have planned a joint dinner also at one of Tom and Tyler's eateries. Steve and Kirsty plan to cook a meal at home. Harry and Clio have made plans to eat with Enrique and Indya at their home. John and Lynda have gone away for the night to Redcoats Farmhouse. Sebastian and Rebecca have gone into town to visit one of the local restaurants.

Josh has gone to get his haircut, but to also catch up with his friend who owns McCarthy's Hair Salon, whilst Judith has gone to get herself some spa treatment.

Josh enjoys a coffee with his friend, then walks through the market square back towards the car park when he bumps into Andrew and Katie. "Hello, you two!" he greets them. "Ah Josh! How are you? Swish hair cut by the way!" as they laugh together and catch up. "So, what are your plans tonight?" Josh asks them. "Oh, not much, just some friends that are coming over" Katie replies. "Josh chuckles and replies, "Friends? Or friendly friends?!". Andrew and Katie laugh as they admit to friendly friends coming over. "Ha-ha, well, enjoy yourselves!" Josh says to them with a smile. "Oh, we will!" Andrew replies with a wink, as the friends hug and say their goodbyes.

Later that evening, Josh and Judith put on their smart clothes and head off to the Hermitage Road Restaurant to take advantage of the meal voucher gift given to them by Dominic and Nicole. After enjoying their meal, they decide to head over to one of the other bars in the town to enjoy some post-meal drinks, when they spot Sebastian and Rebecca also walking across the market square. "Hey, you two, going anywhere nice?" Josh asks them as they all greet each other. "We have just been to the Balcon-du-Lac restaurant" replies Sebastian. "Ah, very swanky!" Judith replies. Rebecca joins in with, "We are just off to get another drink, care to join us?" to which Josh and Judith agree, so the four of them head off to Crescendo's, one of the most upmarket cocktail bars in town.
As the friends enter, Sebastian and Rebecca spot the reverend James and his wife Elizabeth. Rebecca heads over to them both and greets them, followed by Sebastian, Josh, and Judith.
"Ah, hello again!" Rebecca says to them both. The reverend James replies with a smile and gives Rebecca a warm hug as Elizabeth gets up to greet her with a kiss on each cheek.
James then shakes Josh's hand and introduces himself and to his wife Elizabeth.
As Josh goes to shake her hand, she goes in for a hug instead.

"Hello Josh, I have heard about you, and it's a pleasure to finally meet you in the flesh". Josh smiles politely as he awkwardly hugs her back, glancing at Judith who looks back at him with a bit of puzzlement on her face. James and Elizabeth then introduce themselves to Judith, exchanging pleasantries. Finally, Sebastian shakes the reverends hand before turning his attentions to Elizabeth to greet her. She puts on a brave face whilst she gives him a lukewarm hug, but out of the eyes of the others he gives her bottom a gentle squeeze, before whispering in her ear, "Good to see you again Elizabeth". She pulls away gently and just smiles at him, not saying anything in return.

The six of them enjoy a few bottles of champagne and wine, talking and laughing, mulling over world affairs and what is going on in their lives. As the evening draws to a close, plus the fact that they would like to go home and spend some quality time with their respective partners, Josh and Judith are the first to leave, saying their goodbyes with hugs for all of them. As Josh gives Elizabeth a hug goodbye, she leans in and whispers, "It was lovely to meet you Josh, I hope to see you again very soon". As they part from their goodbyes, Josh thinks of what Elizabeth said to him. It wasn't so much the words, but the way that she delivered them. Was she being polite? Or did she emphasize certain words more than they would normally sound? Was she being suggestive he thinks to himself. Josh remains polite and smiles back as he opens the door for Judith as they depart.
The reverend James and Elizabeth are next to leave. As they get up to say their goodbyes, Sebastian and Rebecca stand up to give them both a hug.
As Sebastian hugs Elizabeth, he whispers in her ear, "I think I'll have my tour tomorrow".
Elizabeth then turns her head to Sebastian's ear and whispers back, "There will be no tour tomorrow" as she pulls gently away and smiles at him sweetly.

Sebastian looks at her, slightly annoyed, before pulling his phone out of his pocket, suggesting to her what he has on it, the evidence of her, before adding, "I WILL see you tomorrow" as he puts his phone away, smiling. Elizabeth doesn't react and just smiles sweetly at him as Sebastian and Rebecca leave the bar.

Sebastian and Rebecca head over to the taxi rank to get a lift home but Sebastian realises that he has misplaced his wallet. Searching for it, he realises that he must have left it in the final bar. "Darling, I need to head back to the bar, it must be in there, but if not then I'll check the restaurant" he tells Rebecca. "Can't we just ask the taxi to take us to both? Besides, there are a few dodgy looking people hanging around" she replies. Sebastian smiles at her and replies, "Not really, the town is closed to traffic at weekends don't forget. Don't worry, I'll be ten or fifteen minutes behind. Why don't you go home and slip into something uncomfortable for me?". Rebecca rolls her eyes as she closes the door of the taxi as it departs to take her home.
Sebastian begins to walk back into the town centre, but spotting a small group of rowdy men, he decides to take a different route to avoid them, heading through one of the alleyways.
As he does so, he hears footsteps behind him. "Oi, mate, you've dropped something" comes the voice of someone. Sebastian turns around to see a scruffy, disheveled man approach him.
Sebastian looks at the mans extended hand but sees nothing.
The man then puts forward his other hand to reveal a knife.
Sebastian's eyes look down at the weapon and then back up at the man, with shock and fear in his eyes. "Now give me your fucking phone" the man scowls at him.
Sebastian reaches into his pocket, takes his phone out and slowly goes to hand it to the man.

As the man reaches out to grab the phone, Sebastian quickly pulls his hand back and uses his other hand to grab the man's arm, the one holding the knife.
The two men begin to wrestle as they grunt and groan, trying to overpower each other.
A group of revellers walk past, distracting the two men fighting in the alleyway.
The man lets go off Sebastian and runs off in the opposite direction. Sebastian suddenly looks down to feel that his clothes are warm and wet, raising his hands only to find that it is his blood, and that he must have been stabbed. He tries to shout out for help but finds that he doesn't have the air in his voice to do so, dropping to his knees in panic and fear as he slowly fades away in the shadows of alleyway.

Earlier that evening, whilst still light, two missionaries are walking the roads of Hitchin, spreading the word of their church to anyone who is willing to listen and convert, as they do. "This looks like an inviting house to try" says Elder Daniels. "It sure does brother, I have a good feeling about this one" replies his colleague, Elder Lucas. They approach the house and knock on the door.
"Darling, I think the Wren's are here!" Katie shouts up the stairs to Andrew. "Ah good! Let them in and greet them in the usual way!" he replies. Katie chuckles as she shouts up, "I'm already dresses ready!" she counters. She turns back to walk towards the door to open it, and as she begins to pull the door open, she exclaims, "Who's ready for sex?!". The two missionaries' eyes nearly pop out of their heads as they are greeted by the sight of Katie, wearing stilettos, black fishnet stockings with a black basque and black gloves that go up to her elbows. "Oh! You're not the Wrens! Darling, it's not them!". Katie then asks them, "Would you like to come in?". The two men run for their lives as Katie laughs loudly. "Who was it darling?" Andrew calls down to Katie. "I don't know, but they didn't come in when invited" she replies. "Well, they clearly don't enjoy a sense of fun do they!" he remarks as they both share a cuddle and a kiss whilst laughing.

The next morning, everyone's phones buzz with messages with the news that Sebastian is dead. The friends all text each other, in shock, trying to find out what happened and how it happened. As they try to look for answers, it is already over the local news and social media about the body of a man in his forties has been found.

The wives all try to contact Rebecca, but no answer. She is at home with the police, sobbing her heart out at her loss, being comforted by family members who have rushed over to see her.

"What happened?!"" asks Judith to Josh, "We only saw them last night, this is awful". Josh looks thoughtful and sad as he nods along, trying to make sense of the news.

Dominic is in the market square, in one of the coffee shops, on the phone talking business but also looking over at where the police are, with the area cordoned off with barrier tape and a white gazebo to preserve the scene for clues and evidence. He then calls his wife Nicole to give her an update at what he can see. Phil walks in and sees Dominic and goes over to him to give him a hug, sad at the news of their friend dying. Both men are stoic and talk about the shock of the news.

Just then, Elizabeth walks in through the door. Phil looks up and sees her and gets up to greet her. Dominic looks at them, as he hasn't met Elizabeth yet. Phil gestures for her to join them. As they both walk over to where Dominic is sitting, he cannot help but feel attracted to her, as she is dressed in white ankle stiletto heels, sheer gloss nylons and a floral figure-hugging dress, complete with a small tight cropped black jacket, almost looking quite summery for a winter's day.

"Hello, my name is Dominic" he says to Elizabeth, standing up to greet her. "Hello Dominic, a pleasure to meet you" she replies, smiling and kissing his cheek. Phil offers to buy her a coffee, leaving her and Dominic to get acquainted. "So, do you know what happened over there?" she asks him, referring to the spot where Sebastian met a grizzly end.

"I don't know much I'm afraid" as he looks over pensively.

"I hear you were friends" she replies. "Yes, I, Phil, and a few others know him well". She looks at him with sympathetic eyes and gives her condolences. "Anyway, what about you then Elizabeth? You and your husband are the new couple down our road, correct?". She nods in agreement. "How are you settling in?" he asks her. "Quite well actually, I'm making new friends quite quickly, but I am always looking to make more" she replies. Dominic smiles at her. Phil reappears with a coffee for her as he sits down and joins them in conversation. "So how did it happen? About Sebastian" Elizabeth asks the men. "We think he was mugged and was stabbed in the process" Phil replies. "What a tragedy, to lose a friend, and he was my neighbour too. Rebecca must be devastated" Elizabeth replies. Both men nod in agreement, however, Dominic right now has his mind on Elizabeth, something that she senses. Just then Phil's phone rings. He answers it, stands up and moves into a quieter area to talk to the person on the other end of the call. Elizabeth looks at Dominic and smiles. She picks up her coffee and sips it whilst looking outside, averting her eyes. As she does so she uncrosses her legs for a moment then crosses them again. She can feel his eyes burning into her, watching her, and she senses it as she can see him looking at her through the reflection the window, something her is unaware of. She also knows that he can just about see that she is wearing lace top hold up stockings. She slowly turns her head back to look at Dominic and he turns his eyes slightly away, thinking that he hasn't been caught looking. But she knows, after all, he has gone slightly redder in the face. Just then, Phil returns and apologies for the intrusion of having to take a call. "That's OK, no need to apologise, I was just getting to know your friend" she replies to him. Dominic looks up and just smiles, inside feeling rather hot under the collar but on the outside trying to look calm. Elizabeth gets up and says that she must dash, saying her goodbyes to both men, who stand up to kiss her goodbye. As she walks past the window Dominic watches her, as she turns her head to look through and smile at him. She knows. So does he.

March:
Rampant Easter Rabbits

Dominic is in the coffee shop, working on his laptop and checking his emails and replying to messages on his phone at the same time. Elizabeth comes in through the door, much to Dominic's delight. "Hello again!" he says with enthusiasm as he kisses her on the cheek. Elizabeth smiles broadly as she kisses his cheek and replies, "Hello again, looks like I've made a new friend then!" as they both pull back and sit down. "So, how have you been?" she asks him. He smiles and replies to her that he has been busy with his business dealings and that has been a good distraction from things at home. "What do you mean at home?" she asks him. He looks a little more serious and replies, "Well, I kind of get the feeling that her mind is elsewhere these days". Elizabeth looks at him, sensing an opportunity, and replies, "What do you mean? Do you think she is enjoying herself elsewhere?". Dominic looks at her and replies, "It's possible. I have seen small tell-tale signs but no concrete evidence", then he goes on to tell her how she has dressed up more than usual when going out, being more secretive with whom she texts, and the fact that their love life has taken a nosedive.

"I see" she replies to him. "Well, if she is enjoying herself and you seem to clearly accept it rather than confront it, then maybe you should… enjoy yourself too?" she tells him candidly. Dominic looks at her, thinking for a moment how to reply. He clearly finds her extremely attractive, and he would love to "enjoy" himself with her, but he holds back and does his best to refrain from saying what he is thinking. Finally, he replies to her, "Maybe, but I'm a busy man, my job role keeps me very busy!".

She looks at him with fake puppy dog eyes and exclaims, "Oh you poor man, you really need some down time to relax!".

He looks at her and smiles as he says, "I really wish I could…" letting the words linger as his eyes remain fixed on hers, taken in by her charm.

"But" he continues, "I am off to a conference in London from tomorrow for a couple of nights".
She looks at him and replies with intrigue, "Oh, really? Whereabouts?" to which he replies, "The Mossettes Hotel. It's where the conference is". She begins to stroke her leg slowly then replies, "Really? What a coincidence, I am down there tomorrow too meeting an old friend for lunch. Perhaps we could share a drink after your conference has ended?". She looks at him with a hint of a glint in her eye, suggesting she is taking on board all the information that he is telling her. After a moment of silence, he smiles and tells her that if she is in the area then that would be nice. Elizabeth tells him to take her number, as does she with his number. "Well, that's settles then, I shall see you tomorrow" she declares, as she stands up and heads out of the door of the shop.

The next day, Dominic attends his conference alongside many of his colleagues. During the conference he decides to message Elizabeth. He keeps it lighthearted to begin with, testing the waters of what her humour and personality is like. It doesn't take long for him to find out. After an exchange of messages that turn flirty, she finally ups the stakes and sends him a picture message. Dominic opens the message up to reveal that she has sent an image of the top of her thighs, and her lace top hold up stockings. Dominic nearly coughs his drink up as a colleague next to him in the conference quietly laughs at him.
The conference finally ends, and Dominic has a quick drink at the bar with his colleagues before receiving another text from Elizabeth, which reads, "I have a surprise waiting for you X". Dominic quickly closes his phone as his colleagues continue to talk. "Chaps, I'll catch up with you later, I'm just off to freshen up before dinner tonight". He says his goodbyes and heads off to the hotel lift to take him to the floor that his room is on. As he opens the door to his room, right in front of him, on her knees, wearing only the lace hold up stockings and a large smile, is Elizabeth.

Dominic quickly shuts the door and looks at her, wondering what to say or how to respond, but before he does, she quickly takes his hand and pulls him towards her. He is like a rabbit in the headlights, not quite sure what to do, but he doesn't exactly resist ether. As she pulls him close to her, his waist now inches from her face, she looks up at him and declares, "The patient will see you now Doctor!" whilst removing his trousers, remaining on her knees.

The day arrives for Sebastian's funeral.
All the guests arrive at the church to pay their respects to him and to show their support to his now widow Rebecca. Harry and Clio offer a lift, that is accepted, to the reverend James and Elizabeth. Josh and Judith share a taxi and Andrew and Katie, as the others all make their way either by car or taxi too.
The service is held, and it is an appropriate affair, with speeches from his family and old friends, with his favourite music being played, and the wake being held close by, in Hitchin. At the wake the friends all talk amongst themselves, still finding it weird, strange even, that their friend is no longer with them. As the wives huddle together and drink, the husbands talk amongst themselves and discuss matters away from the sad day. Inspector Matthews and Sergeant Carter turn up, but respectfully wait outside the wake. When the time is appropriate and they spot an opportunity, Matthews walks in and approaches Josh. "Josh, can we talk outside please?" he asks Josh. He is surprised to see Matthews their but smiles, nods, and follows him out. Josh and Inspector Matthews get along well, having moved in similar circles for a few years, they have even gone on bike rides together, there is a respect between the two.
"Mate what are you doing here?" Josh asks him. Matthews looks around to make sure they are along and says, "Mate, between you and I, something doesn't add up with the way Sebastian died".
Josh looks puzzled and asks him, "What do you mean?".

Matthews looks around again before adding, "I've gone through some CCTV footage and we can see that he was followed by someone, the same person with whom he had a fight and lost his life too, but that person was also identified in CCTV at the cocktail bar you guys went to". Josh looks startled as he asks Matthews, "So... do you mean it was planned?!". Matthews looks around again before adding, "It looks that was, it wasn't some random mugging. Josh looks at Matthews and asks him, "Mate, as you know this will never go any further that us two, not even Judith, but why are you telling me this?". Matthews looks at him and declares, "I'm not suggesting anything, but if someone out there is targeting the wealthier people in Hitchin, as in pre-planned, I just want you to be more vigilant that's all, isn't that what mates do?!". Josh smiles and nods in agreement at Matthews. "No, sorry, agreed, thanks mate, it's appreciated". Matthews nods his head and smiles at Josh, then turns to walk away. As he is about to walk out through the door of the venue he turns to Josh and asks, "Bike ride 9am next Friday?". Josh chuckles and gives him the thumbs up and the sign to suggest he will text him more ride details closer the time, then, the two friends part ways.

As the wake finishes, everyone gets into their cars to drive home or wait for taxis to collect them. James and Elizabeth climb into the car driven by Harry. James gets into the front passenger seat so the two men can make small talk. Harry tells James, "That was a lovely service you gave today" before adding, "Not the best circumstances but I thought you did very well". James turns to look at him and thanks him. The two wives in the back, Clio, and Elizabeth, don't talk too much to begin with, but then Clio breaks the silence with, "That was a lovely service today, wasn't it?", being polite in making small talk. Elizabeth turns with a small smile to look at her to agree, before adding, "You look beautiful today, Clio, and I don love that perfume you are wearing too, you 'll have to let me know what it is".

Clio smiles back as she acknowledges the compliments from her recently new neighbour. Elizabeth then moves her hand to stroke the material on Clio's dress to feel what it is. Clio looks a little taken aback at how forward Elizabeth is with personal space, but she too is a forward person, so she does her best to conceal any surprise and pretends as if it is not a thing, having someone practically momentarily stroking your upper thigh via thin material, albeit.

Clio tells her the make and material of the dress, then, once Elizabeth has retracted her hand, Clio looks at what Elizabeth is wearing and decides to do the same thing, to test the waters, who is the alpha female out of these two. Clio decides to reciprocate the question back to her. Clio puts her hand on Elizabeths torso, just below her breasts, and feels the material, asking Elizabeth what her dress is too. As Clio makes small circles trying to guess the fabric, Elizabeth can feel Clio's hand just brushing the underside of her breasts, making her smile. Elizabeth then turns to Clio and looks at her to ask, "Would you like to check any other material?". Clio pauses for a moment before pulling her hands away, not quite knowing what to do. "We're here!" exclaims Harry in the front of the car, as they pull up on to his driveway. The foursome exits the car and exchange handshakes and kisses as they make their way into their respective homes, with James and Elizabeth heading next door. Both front doors open at the same time and the men walk in first, smiling and waving goodbye, followed by the ladies. As they are about the enter, Elizabeth waves and smiles to Clio, who does the same, but then Elizabeth gives Clio a wink as her smile broadens. Clio doesn't know how to react to this, choosing to smile and wave back, to not let anything on. The Queen of Knights Road it seems, has a new power player on the board.

The next morning Harry and Clio say goodbye to each other as she heads to the gym. He gets into his car to drive to town when he notices an item of clothing in the back, a small silk scarf. He doesn't recognise it being Clio's, so he assumes it to be Elizabeth's.

He grabs the item and knocks on her door. Elizabeth answers with enthusiasm upon seeing him. "Hello Harry, what brings you here?" she asks him. "I found this in the back of my car and assumed it was yours" he replies with a smile. She takes the item and thanks him, followed by, "Are you busy? Would you like a quick coffee?". Harry looks at his watch then around and declares, "Sure, I have plenty of time!". Elizabeth shows him into the kitchen where he pulls up a stool to sit on by the kitchen island whilst she makes coffee. "It was a lovely service yesterday, wasn't it?" she tells him. "Yes, a good send off for him really. Poor Rebecca though, she must be feeling terrible though, maybe we should check up on her at some point". Elizabeth smiles and nods as she passes his coffee over to him. "I thought James did a fantastic job too, especially as it was someone he knew, albeit for not very long". Again, she nods in agreement. "Where is he today anyway?" he asks her. "He is working today, long shift too, some christening I think" she replies whilst sipping her own coffee, looking at him. Harry then notices that she is not properly dressed, still in her nightwear, a silk robe that sits above the knee, with the belt done up loosely. Harry is drawn to her legs on display. He then comments, "I take it today is a stay-indoors day then?", testing the waters of what she says next. She smiles at him and replies, "No plans today I'm afraid, just home alone and a bit bored I suppose". Harry smiles at her, thinking about the way she made her comment. Just then his phone rings so he apologies and takes the call.

As he is talking on the phone, casually strolling around the kitchen, Elizabeth loosens the tie around her robe slightly, not enough to be obvious but enough for it to be noticed. Harry concludes his call and turns his attentions back to Elizabeth, and, noticing that her robe is looser, exposing a little more flesh. "For someone who is not going out today you still manage to look glam!" he tells her, paying her the compliment. She smiles at him and replies, "Well, you never know who might be popping in to say hello so it's nice to look my best!" she tells him, sipping her coffee again, but maintaining eye contact.

"So, where is the lovely Clio today then?" she asks him. "She's gone to the gym" comes his reply with a smile. Elizabeth smiles and replies, "I see. Does she go often?". Harry nods and replies with, "She goes most days. I think she spends more time there than at home I think" he replies, making light of the comment. Elizabeth then tells him, "Well, it's clearly paying off, she is a sexy looking woman after all". Harry laughs and says, "True, but looks aren't everything, she can be a nightmare to live with sometimes. Keeping up with the Joneses so to speak!". Elizabeth chuckles as she continues to look at him, her eyes now wandering over his body, a point not lost on Harry. "Would you like another coffee, Harry?" she asks him, to which he nods yes. "I'll just get some more beans to grind, hold on" she replies.

She gets a small step platform out to use so that she can get the coffee beans out from a high up shelf. "I don't know why I keep them so high, probably just making use of the space I suppose" she tells him. As she steps up, she pretends to be a little unbalanced as she reaches up. "Are you OK, do you need a hand?" he asks her.

"I should be fine, but you could just stand behind me just in case I fall!" she tells him.

Harry gets up and moves behind her as she steps on to the highest step to reach up.

"I know they're up here somewhere" she says, not very convincingly.

As she goes on to tiptoes her robe lifts with her as she reaches up too, with the bottom of the robe almost exposing her bottom. Harry stares at her figure, his eyes running up and down her legs, then, he notices than with her robe hem line so high, his thoughts turn to ones of desire for her. She mumbles again about the coffee beans being at the back of the shelf and leans forward more, this time the hem line of her robe lifting higher still. Harry cannot help himself and looks at the top of her thighs, noticing that the robe is the only thing that she is wearing, that she is naked underneath. By now, Elizabeth can feel Harrys hot breath on the back of her legs. She smiles to herself before declaring, "Ah, found them!" as she pulls them into her hand.

"Do you need a hand coming down?" he asks her. She turns her head around from the top of the steps, looks at him with a smile and a glint in her eye as she declares, "I never need a hand going down". Harry instantly laughs and says, "I'll see you down", his remark being construed as courteous but suggestive.

Elizabeth backs down slowly, making sure that she keeps her body close to Harry as she makes the final step back on to the kitchen floor before turning round to face him. She looks at him, seeing that he is clearly turned on by watching her, and says in a lowered tone, "Do you think I still have another level to go before I am down properly?". Harry looks at her with a big grin on his face as she pushes him gently a couple of steps backwards so that his back is pressed against the island.

She lowers herself down to her knees and unbuckles his belt, using her hands to remove his trousers from his waist. She looks once more at him before stating, "I think I am at the right level now". Harry closes his eyes, his back arches against the island with his elbows and arms resting on it for balance as Elizabeth pleasures him.

After a couple of minutes, she slowly stands back up, keeping his gaze fixed on her as she moves to the kitchen table and sits on the edge.

She unties her robe fully, letting it drop to the floor, then commands him to come over. Harry does so willingly, a Cheshire grin over his face as he joins with her and leans in to hold her back to pull her close to him. Harry holds her tight and kisses her passionately as she throws an arm around his back to hold him tight to her, then he buries his head in her neck to pull her in tighter still. As he does so, Elizabeth looks up to the corner of the kitchen, up at the ceiling and stares. Her eyes remain fixed on the small, discreet camera that is there. The question is, is the camera on? Is it recording? She doesn't let on of course, instead, making sure that she revels in the fact that she has seduced yet another man in such a short space of time.
All of this of course is oblivious to Harry, who continues to enjoy the pleasures that she has offered to him.
His arrogance is too strong to think about the repercussions, blinded by his success in the business world, Harry is used to getting what he wants, and on this occasion, he has done so, but was it really him who is the winner here?

Two days later, Harry and Elizabeth text each other to arrange another meeting. Clearly, they must have enjoyed the first encounter, or was it more about the danger and thrill? That evening, Harry tells Clio that he is going out for a quick pint with a potential new client, to which she is used to, so she doesn't question it. Harry pulls out of his driveway and heads down the road a couple of hundred meters, away from his friends and neighbours homes, as to not be seen. As he pulls up quickly, Elizabeth opens the passenger door and climbs in, giggling at the cloak and dagger scenario they are indulging in.
"Where shall we go then?" Harry asks her with a grin on his face. She looks at him with a sly grin and tells him to head for a secluded spot somewhere away from the public. Harry smiles as he starts to drive off, heading to the local nature reserve near the edge of town, about a mile from where they live.

As he pulls up, he checks around to make sure that no one else is around, then turns the engine off. "So, what shall we talk about?" he asks her with a big grin on his face. She looks at him, then seductively bites her lower lip before licking her top lip slowly and gently, looking down at his waist, declaring, "Well, I'm quite pecking so I'll start with this". Harry chuckles as he reclines his chair slightly, allowing her to pleasure him. Unbeknown to the cheating pair, they are in fact not alone, and of all the people too. Enrique browses his phone, texting various people, whilst out walking his dog in the nature reserve. As he approaches the parked car, he narrows his eyes in the near dark and spots that it is in fact Harry's car.
Enrique smiles and is about to call Harry to see where he is, but notices that he can see movement from within the car.
Enrique becomes curious as to why his friend is out in the nature reserve at this time of night, especially as he doesn't own a dog too, so he walks over slowly and quietly, as he is wondering what is going on. Enrique pears through the driver's side rear passenger window, and to his amazement, he sees Elizabeth pleasuring Harry, her head down in his lap, with Harry sat back, oblivious that the two of them inside the car are being watched, not only watched, but by one of Elizabeth recent conquests too, and the fact that they are all friends. Enrique carefully puts his phone on silent and turns the flash off, then takes a few pictures on his phone. At first, he smirks to himself at the situation, but it doesn't take long for him to think that he was the one that was played by her. Enrique then quietly backs away, moving off into the darkness.

The weekend comes and some of the ladies decide to have a girl's night out to Santorini's. Judith, Kirsty, Claire, Maddie, Nicole, Clio, and Elizabeth.
The ladies head to the bar and order their cocktails and find a large enough table to fit them all, talking about the events in their lives from over the past couple of weeks.

Elizabeth is still rather new to the group, so she listens to them, taking on board all the information about their lives that they talk of.

Maddie stands up and asks if anyone would like more drinks, to which they laugh and joke that of course they do. Nicole says that she will help her. Judith announces that she is off to the ladies to powder her nose. As the other ladies still at the table talk, Elizabeth notices Enrique is in the club. A small smile appears on her face, so, not wanting to be obvious, she stands up and follows him, as he walks towards the toilets. "Hello stranger!" she whispers in his ear as he stands outside the toilet doors in the corridor. He turns to see her and smiles and says hello, before turning around again to face the doors of the ladies' cubicles.

She smiles to herself, then steps forward to press her body up against his back, so that she can lean in, to whisper softly, "Would you like to share one of these cubicles quickly?". Enrique turns around smiling, looks her in the eyes and says, "No!". the smile on her face quickly disappears, clearly disappointed at his blunt response, wondering why, but before she can react to his comment, the cubicle door opens next to him, and he greets the lady that exits it. As he smiles at the lady and walks off with her, chatting to her, Elizabeth watches them walk away with just a hint of envy, annoyance almost, but then again who is she to complain? Especially after the activities that she has indulged in recently.

Just then, Judith appears from another cubicle, spotting the waiting Elizabeth and says with a giggle, "I can hear two people in the one next to me making out!", as she walks off, wiping her nose clean from any evidence of what she has been up to, although she did forget to pick up the rolled up twenty pound note that she left on the side of the sink and didn't even wipe the residue powder away. Elizabeth's thoughts though are elsewhere. As she walks off and is about to head in the direction of her table with the other wives, she makes a detour and heads to the VIP booths, clearly curious.

She approaches the bouncer and remarks that she left her bag in one and strokes him arms to apologise, saying that she will be quick. The bouncer nods his head whilst he remains at his spot, watching the main area of the club. Elizabeth walks quickly but carefully to the same cubicle that Enrique took her to. As she reaches it, she can see that the sliding doors are not fully closed, and as she looks through the crack, she can see that Enrique and the lady in question are enjoying themselves in a very familiar way to what she experienced with him in there on the other occasion.

Elizabeth wastes no time and takes her phone out to take a few pics as evidence. Once done, she quickly puts her phone back in her clutch bag and turns, only to see the bouncer standing behind her.

"Come on, you've got your bag, you need to exit the area". Elizabeth smiles at him and thanks him. Elizabeth smirks to herself as she heads back to the table.

"Where are those bloody drinks?" Clio demands with a semi joking tone. Maddie and Nicole appear back at the table carrying everyone's cocktails. "Sorry! The person in front of us made a big order!" Maddie tells them. As the night finally draws to a close, the ladies all make their way homes by sharing taxis.

The next day, Elizabeth is still a little miffed about the way that Enrique spoke to her. Even if he was with another woman, he could have at least been polite, it's not like she wouldn't have understood after all. She decides to text Indya to see if she would like a coffee. Indya replies that she is with the children out in London for the day. Elizabeth decides to see if Enrique is home, and upon spotting his car a few houses down on their road, she decides to pay him a visit. She dresses up smart and sexily for him, as if she was dressed to go out, to let him know what he missed out on and, the fact that she feels very confident in herself too. She knows that men desire her.

She knocks on his door and waits. Enrique opens the door and commands his dog to go back in the house as it playfully dances around his feet in the hallway. "Can I come in?" she asks him. "I don't think so, I am busy" he tells her. "Busy with that woman from last night?" she replies sarcastically. "What do you mean? She is someone I know, a friend" he replies quizzically. Elizabeth looks at him, smiles a knowing smile and replies with a little more seriousness in her tone, "She must be a good friend if she was willing to kneel between your legs in the booth", keeping her eyes fixed on his to gauge his reaction. "I don't know what you mean" he says to her, now serious too. Elizabeth takes her phone out and holds it up, showing him the evidence. "Are you sure I can't come in?" she says forcefully, wanting to have her wicked way with him. This is no longer about sex though; it's a game of power, and who holds the keys to that power.
Enrique becomes annoyed by her actions, leans closer to her and whispers, "You're not the only one who likes to take pictures". She arches backwards slightly, wondering what he meant. She didn't wait long. "I know how much you like to drive into the countryside, especially when Harry is driving!", as he too takes his phone out to show her hi picture. Elizabeth suddenly becomes angry and tries to grab his hand to look closer at the picture, but in a flash, Enrique pushes her backwards to free her hand. "How dare you touch me!" she shouts at him. Enrique laughs as he replies, "That's nothing compared to what you liked in my booth!". She becomes agitated by his comment, and in the heat of the moment, with her phone still in her hand, she then declares, "Perhaps your dear wife would like to know what you have been up to!" as she begins to press buttons on her phone as if to send the picture of Enrique and the lady to his wife Indya.
Enrique reacts without thinking, and quickly leans over to grab her phone from her hand. Elizabeth uses her other hand to grab his face to push him away, and just as she does so, Enrique lashes out and strikes her with the back of his hand, clean on the cheek.

Elizabeth stumbles over as the phone drops from her hand, cracking the screen. Enrique though is still full of rage and stands over her as he says with anger, "If you mention any of this to my wife or anyone, I will have you killed! Do you hear me? You are a no one, a cheap whore". Elizabeth, quite astonishingly, loses the emotions form the moment and gathers herself, quickly standing up and picking up her phone too. She smiles gently at him as she just stands there looking at him for a moment. "Goodbye Elizabeth" he says with a smirk on his face, before closing the door and calling his dog over in the hallway to him. Elizabeth looks at the closed door, smiles, and says to herself, "Goodbye indeed".

The next day, Harry receives a text. It's from Elizabeth, asking if he will come over to help her with something. Harry smirks to himself as he thinks that she is wanting to misbehave. Making his excuses to Clio, he makes his way over to next door. He knocks gently on the front door. Elizabeth answers the door, wearing a long bath robe and leggings, and sunglasses too. Harry is taken aback a little as he was expecting her to look her usual glamorous self. "Hi Elizabeth, is everything OK?" he asks her, looking a little puzzled but not trying to let on his disappointment that this might not be a fun-filled house call for him. "She smiles at him and greets him then asks him to come in. as they enter the kitchen area, she offers a cup of coffee to which he accepts. As they sit down, he asks her, "So what's with the shades? It's not the sunniest of days today!". Before she can reply, Harry notices slight bruising around her cheek and eye area and as he narrows his sight to look closer, he asks her to remove her glasses, to which she does. "What the hell happened to you?!" he asks, shocked at what he is seeing. She looks at him and begins to cry as Harry quickly gets up to comfort her. As she sobs, she says, "It was Enrique". Harry replies with, "Enrique? What happened?".

She tells him, "He got angry with me when I turned his advances down. It was in the club last night. I saw him and went to say hello, he came on to me and when I said no, he grabbed my arm. I pushed him away and he got angry and hit me".

Harry continues to comfort her as he absorbs the information given to him, then as he thinks about it more, he becomes angry at what she has told him. "I am going to have words with him about this" he says angrily. "How dare he hit a woman, the arrogant prick". Elizabeth keeps her head buried in his shoulder, sniffing back tears, but with a hint of a smile on her face. She composes herself as says, "Please don't, I doubt he will remember anything, he was so drunk". Harry replies with, "That's still no excuse. Leave it to me, I will sort him out". Elizabeth gives Harry a cuddle and thanks him for his support, then, she reaches up and kisses him on the cheek, then she kisses him on the lips passionately. Harry puts his arms around her to hold her tight to respond with the same amount of enthusiasm. Elizabeth then moves her hand down and puts it inside his trousers and then looks at him and smiles, adding, "Would you like to go upstairs?".

Harry doesn't need asking twice, as he stands up and holds her hand to follow her up the stairs and to the bedroom.

Easter Sunday.

The next day, Enrique has a home match in London, a cup match against another topflight team. Once he has finished his game and has departed the stadium, he heads home and calls Indya on his car phone to let her know what time he will be home. Enrique ends the call and is about ten minutes away from home when Harry calls him. "Hi Harry, how are you?" he enquires. Harry replies with a stern voice, "Hi mate, I just wanted a word with you about what happened the other night in the club".

Enrique searches his thoughts to think about what he might be talking about, before replying, "Many things happen in that club Harry! Anything in particular?".

Harry responds, "The part where you hit Elizabeth, in particular". Enrique goes quiet for a moment, thinking back, then replies with, "Ah, that was an accident. She tried to grab my phone from me, so I tried to get it back. She fell over in the struggle and must have hit something. It wasn't me Harry". Enrique now is a little worried about that fact that Harry is in the know about his tussle with Elizabeth, but he also thinks to himself to not offer any more information unless asked, as he is curious to know exactly how much Harry knows about him, Elizabeth, and everything that has gone on, especially that he knows what Elizabeth and Harry have also got up to. He bides his time until Harry replies, "Mate, don't play games, you know you hit her, that's bang out of order. Whatever we get up to behind closed doors, you don't hit a woman mate, come on!". Enrique pauses to think before replying, "Harry, I am telling you the truth! She was drunk as hell and when I ignored her and, on my phone, she tried to get my attention by trying to grab it, then she fell". Harry pauses before talking, adding back, "Well, that's not what she told me". Enrique laughs and replies, "And you want to take her word over mine? Besides Harry, you haven't been an angel yourself, have you?".

Harry pauses again on the other end of the line before asking, "What do you mean by that?".

"Oh, come on Harry, you know what I mean, do you forget that I walk my dog often by the nature reserve? It's quite interesting to see what and who you might bump into" Enrique replies. Harry thinks for a moment, thinking back to him and Elizabeth going out to the reserve for some illicit fun, then asks with a tone to suggest he is innocent, "I don't know what you are talking about mate, you'll have to fill me in". Enrique laughs as he replies, "Isn't that what you did to Elizabeth in your car? Fill her in?".

Harry by now has gone quite coy and must think quickly about his reply, but he knows he has been caught out. "You can't prove that mate, that wasn't Elizabeth, that was Clio I was with".

Enrique laughs again then replies with suggestion, "Harry, the pictures on my phone say otherwise. I know what Elizabeth looks like, and I especially know what your wife looks like". Harry reacts quickly and angrily, "You prick, be careful what you say about my wife. And be careful about who you speak to. Watch your back Enrique". Enrique smiles to himself but doesn't reply, choosing instead to hang up the phone.

Enrique pulls up to his house and gets out of his car, opening the boot to grab his sports bag. As he is about to shut the boot he hears a faint noise behind him, like footsteps coming towards him quickly, and as turns around to see who it is, as quick as a flash the last thing he sees is an object coming towards his face, then, he is gone. Enrique loses consciousness as blood begins to pour from a head wound, from an object that has connected with his head. As the dying Enrique lies on the floor, bleeding to death and from suffering a severe head trauma from the blow of the object, the person who hit him rifles through his pockets and takes some personal items, then quickly goes through his car to take a few personal items from it, then, about thirty seconds after that fatal blow was struck, the shadowy figure disappears quietly and off into the darkness.

April:
A Shower of Fools

The next morning, Josh is woken by his phone buzzing with multiple text messages from his friends. He reaches over to grab his phone but before he can open it, Judith comes in, phone in hand, reading the messages that he has too, as they are in the same WhatsApp group. "Oh my God! Enrique is dead!" she remarks to Josh, her voice raised and her face in shock. "Jesus! You are kidding me, right?".

The news of Enrique's death spreads like wildfire. Being a famous footballer, it was only ever going to be big news, national news even, perhaps international news, especially in the world of sport. Judith sends Indya a text to send her condolences but receives no reply, she hasn't even read the message, but the fact that she has just lost her husband, this is no surprise. Judith contacts the other wives to arrange some flowers and card to be sent to Indya's home to let her know that they are all thinking of her in this trying time. That night the national news is dominated by the death if Enrique. The news broadcasters don't give away much information apart from that it looks like a mugging gone wrong. Even Inspector Matthews must go on the TV cameras to give the usual shpiel about enquiries and leads, but deep-down Matthews doesn't truly believe it was a random mugging, especially that it seems too convenient and clean. This is something that he is to later reveal to Josh in confidence.

Two days after the murder of Enrique, Josh takes to the roads on his bike, meeting up with two of his friends that are not in the circle of friends already mentioned so far, Dick and Gerald. As the friend's cycle, they talk about Enrique and theories as to what happened, but that's all they are, just theories.

Dick mentions to them as they cycle, "To be honest Josh, Enrique was quite an arrogant player and person, he must have pissed the wrong person or people off, who knows".

Josh nods and replies that he agrees. "He was a good laugh, but he definitely had an arrogant streak, but not enough for someone to be murdered!" Josh adds.
Gerald also joins in with, "We simply don't know what went on in his life. Maybe it was a mugging, maybe it was something else. Most of the time these things will come out though". As the friends conclude their ride, they pull up in the market square to all go their separate ways home. "Huzzah!" shouts Gerald as he rides off, adding, "Thanks for coming!", leaving Dick and Josh chuckling as they too say goodbye and ride off in their respective directions.

A couple of days later Steve knocks on the Reverend James's door and is greeted by Elizabeth. "Hello, is the man of the house home at all please?" he asks her with a smile. "The man of the house is!" she replies to him, smiling then inviting him in. As Steve enters his eyes wander up and down Elizabeth's body as he follows her down the hallway. As she reaches the kitchen she calls out, "Darling, Steve is here for you". James enters the kitchen and greets Steve with a handshake and offers coffee, to which he agrees and thanks him and Elizabeth. She takes out the cups then asks Steve, "How do you like it? An instant quick one or a slow plunge?". Steve starts to smirk, with a double entendre entering his head, but before he can think of a quick response the Reverend interjects, "She means how do you like your coffee!" with a smirk across his face. Steve is taken aback slightly, appreciating that even though he is a man of the cloth, James does in fact have a good sense of humour, in fact, he didn't seem offended in the slightest. Perhaps he is used to it, he thinks to himself. As the men take their cups to the front room, Steve enters after James, and he looks back into the kitchen, only to be caught looking by Elizabeth, who is looking back at him, and flashes him a cheeky smile and a wink as he walks through the front room doorway.

The two men sit down and start to talk business as the reverend has mentioned to Steve that he is looking to invest some money into businesses and knows that Steve has much experience in this field. Steve talks for about half an hour, giving James advice on what to do and what not to do. Once the business affairs have finished the subject naturally changes to Enrique, to which the two men share their shock at what happened. "Unfortunately, this might be the second funeral I will have to conduct in the space of 6 weeks, and the fact that the two departed souls were friends will make it doubly hard" the reverend tells Steve. He nods at James in agreement and contemplates the information. Elizabeth comes in to join them momentarily to take the empty coffee cups from them both. She leans over the coffee table to pick up Steve's cup, making sure that she leans over more than what is needed, giving Steve an eyeful of her obviously exposed cleavage. As she lifts the cup up, she glances quickly at Steve, catching him looking. Again, she smiles and winks at him, before turning to pick up her husband's cup, giving him a kiss on the cheek before disappearing back to the kitchen. Steve looks a little ruffled and flustered and does his best to hide his embarrassment at being caught having a sneaky look at the reverend's wife, but to his amazement, James chuckles at him and says, "She is a very attractive lady isn't she". Steve looks a little surprised by this but doesn't disagree either. After saying their goodbyes, Elizabeth comes in the front room to say she will see Steve out. As Elizabeth opens the front door, she leans over just enough into Steve to brush her breasts against his chest, pretending to make the hallway narrower than it is. "Do come again Steve, it's not often you get someone who appreciates a slow plunge". Steve smiles at her, replying, "It's the best way to have coffee", as she counters, "Sure, that too…", letting her remark filter into Steve's head to think about. He grins broadly at her as he turns to walk away, telling her, "See you very soon". She watches him walk away and gets her phone out to find his number in the group chat and saves it in her phone properly. For reference later of course.

A couple of days later, Josh and Steve are in the gym, sharing a workout on the machines and cardio equipment, talking about what's been going on that week. "What do you think about the reverend's wife Josh?" Steve asks him. Josh thinks and smiles and replies, "I can't lie mate, she is fit, isn't she?". Steve smiles and he tells Josh about how he thinks she was a bit flirty with him the other day. "Be careful their mate, Kirsty will have your balls!" Josh tells him, sniggering. Steve replies jokingly, "Yeah but wouldn't it be worth it!"

After an hour's efforts, both men take it in turns to fill their water bottles at the water station. Josh goes first then returns to windowsill where their phones are, picking his up to see if anyone has messaged. As he does so, he sees Steve's phone light up with a notification. He sees that Elizabeth has messaged him. Josh quickly looks back at his phone, his eyes turned away from Steve's phone. Steve picks his up to open and wake it and sees that he has a message, that he reads. A small smile appears on his face as he closes his phone. "Last few reps then I must go. Business calls" he tells Josh. "No problem, mate, we've done a good session anyway" Josh replies to him, but Josh is not convinced that Steve is off to take care of business, well, he is but not the usual type of business, Elizabeth business, he thinks to himself.

One hour later, Steve knocks on Elizabeth door. She answers and tells him to come inside quickly, making sure that no one is outside to see. "I saw your message" he tells her. "You said that James wanted me to look at a business he is interested in investing in, correct?". Elizbeth looks at him and smiles and nods, saying, "He's left me in charge to take care of it". Steve smiles back, now thinking to himself if she is being suggestive. He plays along but chooses his words carefully, just in case he is wrong, "So, what does he want me to look into?" he asks her.

Elizabeth walks over to him slowly, and at the same time using her hands to assist her skirt to ride up just enough to reveal her black lace stocking tops and suspenders, replying with one word, "Me!".

Steve's mouth drops as he watches her come close to him, now pressing herself against his body, close enough to feel his breath. She leans over and kisses his neck, using one of her hands to pull one of his hands to her inner thigh to touch her, then using her other hand, putting it down the front of his trousers. "I've seen the way you look at me Steve" she tells him in his ear as she continues to pleasure him. Steve is shaking a little, part of him knowing what he is doing is wrong but at the same time, he finds her such a turn on, not wanting to stop what is going on. "I'm not sure we should be doing this" he tells her, his conscience kicking in a little, but not enough to stop her fully and pull away. "You will find that I am extremely discreet, I promise no one will ever know" she tells him. In the history of the world, how many people have heard that line before?! Exactly. But clearly Steve is too far gone in the excitement of it all and carries on. Elizabeth slowly goes down to her knees and takes his trousers down to pleasure him, looking up at him the whole time, then after several minutes she stands back up and perches herself on the table to let her skirt ride all the way up to her waist, beckoning him over to return the favour. Steve obliges and moves himself into position to do so. After she is satisfied enough, she begs Steve to take her there and then on the table. He is not asked twice. As they are in the throes of sin, Steve's phone begins to ring, it is Josh, trying to get hold of him. He ignored the first attempt, but Josh tries again, so Steve uses the auto reply function on his phone to send a message to Josh. The phone doesn't ring again, as Steve and Elizabeth conclude their activities.

The next morning, Judith and some of the wives meet up to go for a jog together. Joining Judith is Kirsty, Claire, and Maddie. The hot topic of conversation is the recent passing of Enrique, who is still making headlines as the investigation goes on.
"Has anyone heard from Indya recently?" Judith asks the group, as they run through the local countryside trails along the greenway.

Kirsty replies, "No, nothing. I have text her, but I don't think she has read it". "Same here, nothing back yet" replies Claire. "I hope she is OK" adds Maddie. The ladies continue their run, heading into Willian village and past The Fox pub and the local church. As they do so, Judith changes the conversation to the reverend James and his wife Elizabeth. "So, then ladies, what do we think of the recent additions to the crew?". Kirsty laughs and says, "I cannot lie, I think James is quite fit personally" which makes the other ladies giggle, nodding their heads in agreement. Maddie adds, "Elizabeth is quite an attractive lady don't you think?". The others nod to agree, followed by Kirsty saying, "She seems nice, but…". The others wait for her to finish the sentence, which prompts them to ask, "Go on!", to which she continues, "Well, it might just be me, but I think she is a little flirty with the men, just saying". Judith replies, "I haven't been in her company enough to judge yet, but I wouldn't rule it out!". Maddie counters, "We should give her a chance, maybe she just wants to build friendships, they are still quite new to the area and our group might intimidate her a bit? I'm happy to get to know her a bit more". Claire pipes with, "God, imagine Katie saying that! We know how that would end!", which sends the group of ladies into fits of laughter.

It's the weekend and it is the men's turn to go on their run. They meet up with the other runners at the club and all chat and discuss what they have been up to over the past few days, well, maybe some of them don't exactly reveal all details, especially those that have been involved with extra-marital affairs with certain persons.
Josh, Geoff, Andrew, Tom, and Tyler all run together and talk about the recent events surrounding Enrique. Some of the other club members join them in the conversation as they all speculate on what happened. As the group begins to stretch out as each runner finds their chosen pace along the countryside route, Josh finds himself running next to Andrew, or more so, Andrew made sure he ran beside Josh. "So, what have you been up to this weekend or need I ask?!" Josh asks Andrew whilst smirking at him.

Andrew chuckles as he begins to tell Josh about his and Katies visit to a local swinger's club, that is about half hours' drive north on the A1. "Standard night?" Josh asks him. Andrew is quite candid about his and Katies sexual activities together, and he is happy to talk about it to his closest friends. And volunteer the information he does. Andrew replies to Josh with a smile, "It was the monthly themed night that they hold, you know, a bit of dress up!". Josh laughs as he continues to listen to his friend. Andrew continues, "It was vicars and tarts night, nothing unusual there I suppose, but, whilst the party was in full swing...", to which Josh laughs and quickly interjects with "No pun intended!". Andrew laughs but doesn't break stride in his conversation. "Whilst everything was going on in various places around the club in its rooms and areas, I saw a couple that looked quite similar to James and Elizabeth". Josh looks at Andrew and laughs, telling him that surely it couldn't have been. "Well, it was dimly lit, and it was hard to tell for sure, but if it was our new reverend friend, he had the perfect outfit!". Josh laughs again as he listens to Andrew, who adds, "I know I haven't seen much of them. If it was just one of them, I wouldn't bat an eyelid, but our reverend looks like he's in good shape, and his wife Elizabeth is in good shape!". Josh nods in agreement as they both acknowledge with a nod and a chuckle about how good looking physically Elizabeth is. "Besides, I probably did have a bit too much Charlie and Katie was being kept quite busy too" Andrew adds, as Josh laughs. "Well, do we have a swinging vicar amongst our flock?" Josh asks and laughs at the same time. Andrew replies with a wink, "I'll find out next time if it's her!".

Whilst the men are out running, some of the other husbands who do not run at the club are out at other clubs with their children. Some are at football, some rugby, some hockey. Most other wives are with them. Except Clio. She knows that the reverend James will be at church, that Harry is at football with the kids, and that Elizabeth doesn't have children.

She sees this as a chance to speak to Elizabeth and to assert a little authority back, especially as she feels like Elizabeth had taken some of her alpha power away from her when they were in the back of the car recently.

Clio gets ready, glamming herself up so that she looks her best, not wanting to be outdone by her neighbour, then takes the very short journey out of her driveway and onto Elizabeth's, knocking on her front door.

Elizabeth answers the door and is surprised to see that it is Clio. "Oh, hello!" she exclaims looking surprised, wondering why she has come over unannounced. In all recent meetings it has been planned when they have all met up for a variety of reasons, but this time Clio wanted to wrestle a little bit of her alpha female power back, but not that the other ladies would have seen it being taken, to Clio it was of a personal thing. But something also twigged inside her mind about Elizabeth that intrigued her, thinking back to the incident in the back of the car. Was it her inner power that she wanted to assert back? Or was it something else? Did she feel like she had dressed up to impress and show who was the more beautiful woman? Or was it dress to impress for something else? Clio thought about these things, but she dismissed them as she walked through the door.

"Coffee?" Elizabeth asks Clio. "Do you have a non-caffeine herbal tea? I am trying to be good" Clio replies. Elizabeth looks at her and with a wry smile reply, "Sure" as she fumbles in a cupboard to find some. As the two ladies sit down on the sofa they begin to talk about recent events, making small talk about what they have been up to this week and other newsworthy stories and topics. Clio then asks Elizabeth if her and James have plans to start a family. "Not any short-term plans, besides, as much as I love children, I do enjoy my freedom". Clio replies with, "Well I do envy the chance to do whatever and whenever sometimes". Elizabeth looks at her and replies with, "As in doing something spontaneous when the mood feels like it?". Clio looks at her, catching the way she is being looked at, the same way that Elizabeth had looked at her when she got out of the car that time recently.

Clio pauses for a moment, feeling slightly nervous as to what Elizabeth means, excited almost, but Clio being Clio and not wanting to be outdone, she puts on a front. "If we want to go out, Harry and I, we always find a way" she tells Elizabeth, who smiles sweetly, followed by her asking Clio, "And what about sex?". Clio pretends to be a little shocked at this and laughs then replies, "Elizabeth! We find time for that too". Elizabeth asks, "So you have a healthy drive then?". Clio nods and smiles and murmurs in agreement. Elizabeth then asks, "And do you try new things together? You know, to keep it spicy".

Clio shuffles where she sits, trying to look relaxed and in control, but it is Elizabeth now in control of the narrative. "Well, Harry can sometimes be a bit too quick to the point, as in not spending too much time on the build up so to speak, if you know what I mean". Elizabeth now spots an opportunity to pull on that thread of conversation. Elizabeth then says, "You know, men can be like that sometimes. It's sooo frustrating! Sometimes you just want to enjoy some gentle, then passionate kissing. Lots of stroking and caressing. Do you know what I mean?". Clio does. Just listening to Elizabeth talk is making her shuffle again where she sits. Elizabeth shuffles a little closer to Clio and then puts her hand out to feel the material of her skirt. "I must confess Clio, you always look so glam, so beautiful when I see you" as she continues to feel the material. Elizabeth is using this opportunity to see how Clio responds. Clio doesn't stop her. Elizabeth can sense and see that Clio is now nervous, her mouth ever so slightly open and her breath slightly elevated. Elizabeth has seen this look before, from her own quite extensive experience. She then moves her hand lower to stop touching the skirts material and puts it on Clio's upper thigh instead, using the smooth side of her fingernails to gently stroke Clio's thigh. "Are you OK?" she asks Clio, who looks down at Elizabeth hand, as she has a hint of a smile on her face and nods gently. Elizabeth then shuffles right next to Clio, then uses her other hand to take hold of Clio's cheek to turn it towards hers, then Elizabeth slowly leans in to gently kiss Clio on the lips.

This sends a shudder through Clio's body, making her nervous but very excited at the same time. She has never done this before, but right now she doesn't care. She is not thinking about Harry or anyone or anything else as she allows Elizabeth to kiss her. Clio responds by opening her mouth to passionately kiss Elizabeth back. Now both ladies fully embrace as their hands hold and wrap around each other in a clinch, using their hands to continue to stroke each other's bodies, enjoying the new experience together.

As they explore each other, Elizabeths hand moves to the upper most of Clios thighs, then begins to pleasure her as they continue to kiss. At this point, whilst Clio is beginning to moan with pleasure, Elizabeth stops kissing her then moves off the sofa and onto her knees. She pushes Clio's legs open and begins to kiss her inner thighs, moving her mouth slowly upwards, inch by inch, until she reaches the top, using her mouth to pleasure Clio in a way she has not experienced from another woman before. At that moment, Clio relaxes even more.

For a fleeting moment her thoughts turn to Harry and that she is misbehaving with someone else, but in her mind, she quickly justifies it by thinking to herself that it isn't with another man so it doesn't count, besides, she believes that if Harry knew or found out, he would be turned on by knowing that she was with another woman. but she is too far gone to care right now. After several minutes and an explosive ending, Elizabeth finishes her actions and moves her head upwards to kiss Clio passionately. The two embrace again, then Elizabeth asks Clio, "Have you ever tasted another woman before?". Clio looks at her nervously before shaking her head to suggest she has not. Elizabeth takes her place again on the sofa and uses her hands to encourage Clio off the sofa and onto her knees. Clio looks on a little nervously. This is new territory for her after all. "I want this so badly" Elizabeth tells Clio, reassuring her. Elizabeth then parts her legs and uses a hand to pull gently on the top of Clio's head to motion it to return the favour that she has just given Clio. Elizabeth smiles wryly to herself as she leans back and enjoys.

May:
Picture Displays & Come What May

It's the first weekend in May and everyone is preparing for the annual town 10km race. Josh is busy helping his team to set up the course whilst some of the other friends are enjoying a coffee and lunch at Redcoats farmhouse, just outside of Hitchin. The day is busy for most of them as they prepare in their own way for the event as some have children's clubs to also attend whilst every day homelife continues. Once the course is set up Josh heads into town to make sure that all the equipment needed for the next day is ready, and to answer any last-minute messages from the participants.

That evening, when home, Josh and Judith are paid a visit by the reverend James and his wife Elizabeth. "Hi James, Elizabeth, to what do we owe this pleasure?" asks Judith as she greets them at her door. James replies, "Hello Judith, we just wanted to pop by to see how you both were and to thank Josh for his efforts towards tomorrow's event, especially for taking the church into consideration in his plans, I know the local clergy are happy about it and are supportive". Judith invites them in to see Josh and offers them both a drink, as they sit down to chat. Elizabeth as usual is looking very smartly turned out whilst James is looking casually dressed. "We haven't really had much chance to catch up with you both so we thought we would stop by on our way out to say hello and to thank you for your efforts regarding tomorrow" Elizabeth tells Josh. He replies with, "That's no problem at all, a pleasure". Elizabeth then asks Josh, "Tell me, do you still need any help with volunteering duties?". Josh replies that any help is always appreciated. She agrees to help as Josh outlines what she can do to help. James asks Judith about the house so she offers to show him around for a tour, especially as Josh will be talking shop about the event. "So once the tail end runner has gone past, are you OK to help take the signs down?" Josh asks Elizabeth. "Oh, that's no problem, I'm good at taking things down" she replies quite suggestively to him.

Josh chuckles at the comment but doesn't follow it up, staying on track, even though he can feel Elizabeth's eyes are on him, as she shuffles a little closer to him as he shows her the map of the course. Judith and James arrive back in the living room to conclude the mini tour. Once they have finished their drinks, Judith accompanies James and Elizabeth to the door to see them out. "See you tomorrow Josh nice and early" Elizabeth tells him. "Thanks again for agreeing to help" he replies to her, as they leave. Once the door is shut, Judith asks Josh what he thinks of James and Elizabeth. "They seem nice enough. I must admit, I think she is a little bit flirty!". Judith replies that she thinks so too. "Did you behave yourself?!" she teases him, knowing that most men would find Elizabeth very attractive. "Of course! Who needs beef when I have steak, right here with me!" Josh replies with a wink and a smile. "Come on, let's go upstairs and put on a naughty movie" she tells him, groping him to let him know she is feeling a little playful.

The next morning the town centre starts to get busy with participants of the race filling the square. Josh makes sure that all his volunteers are in place and ready to go by calling and texting them. Phil and Dominic turn up and ask Josh if he needs any help with the event. "You could help with Elizabeth's position if that's OK Phil? That spot could do with two people". Dominic silently feels awkward as he was hoping not to be asked to help at Elizabeth spot, maybe regretting what he did with her, then quickly asking Josh to help him in the square. "Sure, no problem" Josh replies to Dominic. Phil smiles and replies that he will do so. Josh then asks Phil and Dominic "Maddie and Nicole not running today then?". Phil replies, "Sadly not, Maddie's not feeling well so she's resting so I thought I'd come and help". Dominic also replies with, "Same for Nicole. We were all together last night so it must have been the drink or something we ate, but us men are sturdy stuff, so we are here!" Josh smiles and thanks them both. Phil then heads off in his car to where Elizabeth will be as Dominic stays with Josh to help in the market square.

As the race starts and all the runners set off, they are cheered on by various people across the course.
Most of the other friends are taking part.
As Harry collects a water cup from the Bird in Hand pub in Gosmore, he notices Elizabeth is marshalling with Phil. Whilst he doesn't suspect anything, a small pang of jealousy comes over him as he sees them, but he manages to not let this be seen.
Phil cheers for him then turns to clap and cheer other runners, but Elizabeth keeps her gaze fixed on him, blowing him a small kiss and a wink to go with it.
Harry smiles, winks back, and runs on. As the other runners are continuing to go past them both, Phil compliments Elizabeth on looking so glam for a sports event. "I think you must be the most glamourous volunteer here today!" he tells her. She thanks him and replies, "I do enjoy it, I'm always up for dressing up". Phil smirks as he continues to clap the runners. Elizabeth spots his smirk as and flashes him a look and a knowing smile. He looks at her for a moment, smiling, before they both return to the event.

The following day it's the Early May Bank Holiday. Some of the friends decide to go for a walk to the Fox in Willian, one of their preferred destinations, plus it's a good excuse to stop off for a drink and to be active. Josh, along with Judith, Andrew, Katie, Geoff, Claire, Tom, Tyler, Phil, and Dominic
As they walk along the countryside trails, they pass through a small car park in the woods. Most of the friends are talking and not paying much attention to their surroundings, but Phil spots Harry's car, parked, almost tucked away at the back of the car park. His car is not hard to miss as he has a private number plate. Phil sees that it is empty and wonders where Harry is. Phil calls out to the others that he will catch them up as he is just having a wild wee in the bushes.
As he approaches the car, he spots on the passenger seat an accessory of clothing and a handbag in the footwell.

For a split moment he thinks that Harry and Clio must be in the countryside somewhere, then he quickly remembers that Clio is not even around as he remembers her saying in their WhatsApp group that she was taking the children to a show in London for the day. It is then it dawns on him that he recognises them, and that these items belong to Elizabeth.

He remembers her wearing that style of scarf yesterday, with its distinct pattern, and she had that same bag too. He remembers because he paid her a compliment about the way she looked. He starts to think about it, then begins to put two and two together, thinking back to past events and how Harry and Elizabeth have interacted when they have been at gatherings. Phil quickly looks around him to see or spot them. He doesn't see anything, so he begins to walk away, only to hear a few snapping twigs and rustling of undergrowth. He quickly does a U-turn and tiptoes to where the sounds are coming from, peering through a gap in the trees and bushes. In the near distance, about thirty meters away, he spots two people kissing passionately and lots of groping. He quickly makes them out. It is Harry and Elizabeth. Phil's jaw drops as he watches them, amazed at what he has discovered. He watches on as Elizabeth then opens Harry's trousers and pulls then down, followed by her dropping to her knees, about to perform a sex act on him. "Phil?" someone shouts out to him. loud enough for him to hear but not loud enough for Harry and Elizabeth to hear, as they are too far away. Phil quickly departs and catches up with the others, smiling to himself, the cogs in his head turning.

The rest of May is rather uneventful for most of the friends, although Elizabeth continues to secretly meet with Harry on occasion. Clio and Elizabeth have also met up again, to experience the same situation they did the previous month. Steve has also managed to meet up with Elizabeth again too, secretly meeting at a hotel to indulge in extra marital affairs. Phil though bides his time with the information that he has in his possession, having witnessed Harry and Elizabeth in the woods on the early Bank Holiday.

Near the end of the month, Rebecca, the widow of Sebastian, is paid a visit by the police. Inspector Matthews, along with sergeant Carter, are leading the case for her husband's murder, as they talk to her to update her on any progress about the incident. "I am sorry that we haven't found the suspect yet. We simply don't have enough evidence to pin it on anyone as the DNA we found doesn't match anyone on our database". Rebecca is annoyed about the news but shows sympathy towards his efforts too. "I promise you I will continue this investigation until I do. I also came to return his phone as we didn't find anything to suggest a motive". Rebecca thanks them and says goodbye to Matthews and Carter as they depart. Rebecca sits down and opens the phone to view it, thinking of her late husband, scrolling through the pictures. She notices that the last few days before he died were missing, thinking that odd as she knows he is always on his phone taking pictures of anyone and anything. She flicks through the options and finds another file that when she opens it, she finds more pictures and videos.

It is then that she notices that there are pictures of Elizabeth with Enrique, at first a picture of them smiling and drinking in a private booth, then one of them kissing, followed by a picture of her performing a sex act on him, all in Santorini's. she then sees the video that Sebastian had filmed of Elizabeth being quite violent towards the man who ended up in a coma in hospital. She then sees the pictures of Elizabeth and Steve alone on her house, also one of them looking rather cosy too.

Rebecca is shocked by everything that she has seen, her mind starts to think about what she has seen, knowing that her husband did like to gossip too, but why would he not tell her about this? She then starts to scroll through his old messages and finds one that was sent to Elizabeth. There is only one message, with no reply from her too. All it reads is "Think about what I said".

Rebecca starts to try and put the pieces together. She has seen pictures of Elizabeth and Enrique cheating on their partners.

She has seen Elizabeth being violent in a video. She has seen Elizabeth in her home alone with Steve.
To conclude she has seen a text, which was dated last out of the evidence, from her own husband to Elizabeth. Rebecca thinks to herself about it all. She concludes that she is not bothered about the Elizabeth pictures and video, although she now thinks of her as someone with the morals of an ally cat. But what bothers her the most is the text message that Sebastian sent to Elizabeth. She whispers to herself, "What does this mean? What were you up to?". After some thinking, the curiosity gets the better of her. Rebecca puts her late husband's phone in her pocket and heads over to speak to Elizabeth in person. She knocks on the door, her face quite stern and ready to have a confrontation, only for James to answer the door instead. Rebecca's face quickly softens as she asks if Elizabeth is about so that they can have a catch up. "Hi Rebecca, how are you? I'm sorry, she is not here this week, she has gone to visit some family back in Hampshire". "Oh… that's Ok, it was just a catch up" she replies to him, looking a little dejected that she hasn't had the meeting that she wanted, to confront Elizabeth. She doesn't make an issue of it in front of him and departs. Upon arriving back home, Rebecca cannot stop thinking about the situation and decide to call Elizabeth.

"Hi, Elizabeth, its Rebecca" she says down the phone. "Hi Rebecca, how are you?" Elizabeth replies. "Fine, just fine, listen, I wanted to see you in person as I wanted to speak to you face to face". Elizabeth pauses for a moment before replying, "Really? Is everything OK?". Rebecca pauses then says,

"The police returned Sebastian's phone to me today, and, well, let's just say that I have found some rather revealing content". A silent pause follows, then finally Elizabeth breaks the silence with, "Oh, I see. Are you free tomorrow? Would you like me to come and see you?". Rebecca replies with, "I think that would be a good idea, don't you?". Elizabeth and Rebecca agree upon a time, and they end the conversation.

The next day Elizabeth arrives at Rebecca's home where she greets and lets her in. the two ladies head to the kitchen where Rebecca offers Elizabeth a drink. Rebecca's posture and emotions are prickly, almost ready to have a confrontation with Elizabeth, who, on the other hand, seems to be quite relaxed, maybe having had twenty-four hours or so to prepare for this meeting.
"So, as you know I wanted to speak to you about our conversation yesterday" Rebecca tells her. Elizabeth smiles gently as she nods and replies that she is happy to talk about things. Rebecca continues, "Look, we are all adults, and whatever we do in life, we accept the results or consequences". Elizabeth replies to her, "In what respect do you mean?". Rebecca's face changes as she becomes a little annoyed at Elizabeth's response, trying to look and sound innocent. Rebecca adds, "Look, if you want to sleep with Enrique, that's between you too, although Indya is my friend. If you want to sleep with Steve, that's up to you too, and I am sure there's a reason for hitting the man in the club too…". Before she can finish, Elizabeth cuts in quickly, "Look, Rebecca, yes Enrique and I did have a one-off thing. He's a famous footballer and I was attracted to him in that respect. As for Steve, nothing happened there, he just came over to say hello…" Rebecca's face suggests she doesn't believe a word Elizabeth is saying. Elizabeth continues, "The man in the club started a fight and caught me in the scuffle so I lashed out to defend myself". Again, Rebecca doesn't look impressed. "That's not what I saw in the video Elizabeth" she replies. Elizabeth replies with, "Well, if there is footage then it doesn't show how it started".
Rebecca pauses for a moment to take on board and think about what Elizabeth has said. On the outside her face is saying "I am listening and considering what you have said could be true" but inside her head she is thinking, "You are a lying hussy".
Rebecca finally breaks the silence with, "Look, I don't overly care much about those pictures and video. Your dirty little secrets can stay just that".

Elizabeth smiles and looks at the floor, almost smiling. "There is one thing though that does bother me the most", at which point Elizabeth's wry smile disappears as she looks back up at Rebecca. "My husband sent you a text, saying, *think about what I said*. What did he mean by that message? Why are there deleted messages too?". Elizabeth tries to look convincing by replying that she doesn't know. "Don't play games Elizabeth, I think I've seen enough of your character now to know that you are not exactly an angel by a long way". Elizabeth's demeanour now changes, her posture becomes upright as she stares at Rebecca. "Do you really want to know?" she says to Rebecca, also staring back, gazed fixed, waiting for the answer. Elizabeth then speaks, "He wanted to sleep with me, try to blackmail me into bed because of the pictures and video". Rebecca's face changes to one of shock and disbelief. "No, he's not like that Elizabeth" she tells her. "My husband wasn't like that" she continues, now getting angry at what she has been told. Elizabeth sighs, then pulls out her phone, scrolls through some messages then shows them to Rebecca:

Seb - "Think about what I said".

Liz – "I'm not interested".

Seb – "Well then, maybe your secrets will no longer be that then?"

Liz – "And what if I say yes?".

Seb – "Then your secrets will stay as they are".

Liz – "What do you want?".

Seb – "I want you in your stockings and suspenders".

Liz – "You can have a picture to play over, that's all".

Seb – "No, in person. No pictures. I want the real thing. They did. You are going to drop down to your knees and blow me. Then we will sixty-nine on your bed".

Liz – "I will think about it".

Seb – "There is nothing to think about. You will go on all fours whilst I enjoy taking you from behind. I will pull on your hair and you will moan to show me just how much you are enjoying it, and you will enjoy it".

The messages then stop.

Rebecca looks at Elizabeth as she sits back, her eyes beginning to fill with tears as she begins to sob at what she has just read. Elizabeth looks at Rebecca and puts her hand out to console her but as she strokes Rebecca's arm, Rebecca quickly reacts and slaps Elizabeth across the face. Her tears quickly stop as she becomes angry again. "You were willing to sleep with my husband to keep your filthy little secrets, weren't you?". Elizabeth replies with, "No! I never planned nor was I willing to do so". Elizabeth continues, "Look, I know you are angry with me about this, I don't blame you, but I promise I was never going to do anything with Sebastian". Rebecca softens as she has come to realise that her husband was in fact implying that he was willing to blackmail Elizabeth to sleep with her. "I can't deal with this right now. I want you to go". "I understand. Please, don't mention this to anyone" Elizabeth asks of her. Rebecca looks up and says, "I'll think about it" giving Elizabeth a stern stare, repeating her words to her late husband. "Before I go, can I use your bathroom please?" she asks Rebecca, who replies with monotone, "Up the stairs, second door on the left". Elizabeth walks up the stairs, noticing the bare wooden floors and how steep and how many steps to climb there are, watching her footing as she does so.

On her return, Elizabeth sits down on the sofa whilst Rebecca mulls over what she has read and what Elizabeth has said to her. "I think its time you left" Rebecca tells her. Elizabeth silently gets up and begins to leave. "For what its worth, I am sorry Rebecca. If it helps, I would never do anything that the messages said". Rebecca doesn't respond as she shows Elizabeth out through the front door. As Elizabeth steps out, Rebecca begins to speak, making Elizabeth turn to face her.

She says, "You know, isn't it funny how my husband and Enrique now happen to be dead, and you are the common denominator in this sordid episode". Elizabeth looks down at the floor, knowing that if she replies then it will lead to an all-out argument, so she chooses to remain silent, as she turns back around to walk off to her home next door.

Elizabeths phone rings. She takes it out to answer it, speaking to the unknown caller. She speaks, "Hi… yes… not very well… she now suspects that I had something to do with her husband's murder… yes, I know…OK… If you think so… OK bye" as she hangs up. Elizabeth reaches her own driveway and as she approaches her front door she looks over at Rebecca's house, spotting that she is looking out through one of her windows, staring at Elizabeth. Elizabeth doesn't respond or show any emotion as she looks back for a moment before disappearing into her home.

Rebecca heads to her front room and gets Sebastian's phone out again to go over the images and video, looking for anything that she may have missed. As she looks again at the pictures of Elizabeth with Steve in her house, she decides to call him. "Steve, it's me, can I see you in person to speak to you about something please?". Steve replies that he is busy but will pop by later that day to see her. She thanks him and hangs up, pondering what she will say, what she will ask him. Does she try to play it cool and see if he will volunteer any information? Rebecca then looks at her phone and ponders whether to call the police to report the information and knowledge that she has gained from her meeting with Elizabeth, but she decides to wait to speak to Steve first. As she gets up to walk into another room, out the corner of her eye she spots the figure of something or someone from a distance looking into her window, staring at her. She is surprised and becomes anxious, but she does her best to try and focus on who or what is looking at her. She quickly pulls her phone out to call the police but as she looks back up the figure has vanished from her sight. She rushes to the window to look around, but no one can be seen.
She rushes outside to see if anyone is there but cannot see anyone. As she looks around and is about to turn and walk back in her house, the front door slams shut. She quickly rushes to the back door that's open and enters her home. The front door slam again. She checks the house, but it's empty. By now though she is afraid.

June:
Long Days and Nights Can Be Murder

June. The month with the longest daylight hours in the year, and one that the friends take advantage of with gatherings and events, but, not without its pitfalls.
Josh is busy having new solar panels and a new car charging point installed onto his home by SOMA, the Solar PV, Battery Storage, EV charging points company. As the company install his new purchases, his phone begins to ring, seeing it is Rebecca, he answers it. "Hi Rebecca, how are you getting on?" he asks her. "Hi Josh, not too bad thank you, but I do have a couple of questions I'd like to ask you" she asks him. Rebecca then goes on to ask him about the night that Sebastian died. "Elizabeth and James were with us quite late I think, when we were all in town, why what's up?" Josh replies to her, intrigued and puzzled about why she is asking about Elizabeth in particular. "Oh, it's nothing, just having an off day and trying to make sense of it all that's all". Josh reassures her and asks if she would like to join them for dinner to cheer her up.
Meanwhile, in town at Wisbey Osteopathy, Judith is in the waiting area for her appointment. Her phone rings, it is Kirsty.
Judith – "Hi Kirsty, how are you?".
Kirsty – "Hi Judith, all good thanks. Are you still coming out to lunch tomorrow?".
Judith – "Yes, looking forward to it".
Kirsty – "Oh, by the way, I've got some juicy gossip for you" a friend was in Santorini's the other night and two women were escorted of the premises as they were caught in the toilets having sex with each other!".
Judith – "Oh my word! Anyone we know?"
Kirsty – "I don't know, my friend said they had their heads bowed low so they couldn't be recognised".
Judith – "Well there's always something going on it that place it seems!".
The ladies conclude their conversation.

Meanwhile, Clio is having her hair coloured and styled at McCarthy's. "Got any nice plans coming up Clio?" Steve asks her. Clio replies with, "Just the usual stuff for the half term with the kids, holidays planned for July and August, the usual" as Steve continues his work. Just then, her phone pings with a message. It is Elizabeth, writing to ask if she would like to meet up. Clio smiles wryly to herself as she replies to the message, organizing a date to do so. Whilst Clio is out, Harry is at home and gets a knock on the door. "Hi Phil, a nice surprise to see you, want to come in?" he asks Phil. "Sure, how are you? Home alone today?" Phil replies, seeing and knowing that Clio is not home as her car is not on the drive. The two men head to the kitchen and Harry makes Phil a coffee whilst they make small talk, before Phil changes the mood of the conversation. "A few of us went on a nice walk recently to The Fox, and I saw your car parked up in the woods nearby. I did pop over to see if you were there, but it was empty" Phil says. "Oh really? When was that?" Harry replies, his mind racing to think when he was last there, then it suddenly dawned on him why he was there. Phil then smiles and replies, "I can't remember the exact date, but it's what I saw that intrigued me". By now, Harry is starting to look a little uncomfortable, knowing full well what he was there for, but confident enough to try and talk his way out of it. "What do you mean?" Harry asks him. "Well, you were not exactly alone" Phil replies, now smiling a bit more obviously at Harry. "Harry, I saw you, both of you! I saw Elizabeths possessions in your car and when I heard a noise, I saw you and Elizabeth in the woods, and well, let's just say that she was giving you quite a treat!". By now the colour in Harry's face has drained at the realisation that he has been caught out. Phil, still smiling asks him about it all, to which Harry tells him it was a one off. "Really? Are you sure about that?" Phil teases. The power of this debate is clearly in the hands of Phil. "Mate, please don't say a word to anyone about this, please?" Harry asks him, almost begging. "Your secret is safe with me mate" Phil tells him, still with a smirk on his face. After the two friends have finished talking about the situation,

Phil says his goodbyes and exits the house. As he walks along the road towards his car, he looks at Elizabeths home and he decides to pay her a visit, so he knocks on her door. "Hello Phil. How are you?" she asks him. "Good, very good indeed, thank you" Phil replies, smirking almost. Elizabeth invites him in. As they sit in the kitchen with a drink on the sofa, they make small talk about what they have been up to recently. Then Phil changes the subject to what he saw. "By the way, I saw you with Harry recently. In the woods. In Willian". Elizabeth looks slightly shocked by this and tries to explain as an innocent walk as they are neighbours. "And do you always drop down to your knees and bob your head back and forth to catch up with a neighbour?" Phil tells her, a wry smile on his face. Elizabeth knows that what he has said is true and doesn't even bother to try and make any more excuses. "Fine. You are clearly a smart man Phil, so I won't try to hide it from you" she tells him, almost with a smile on her face though. Phil sees this and it makes him wonder if she doesn't care or has something else on her mind. Phil turns on the sofa to face her better. "Don't worry, I won't tell anyone, I'm very good with secrets" he declares, and in a quite suggestive way too. Elizabeth smiles sweetly as thinks quickly about what to say next. "That's very kind of you Phil. Tell me, how can I thank you?". Phil looks away to think then turns back to face her, replying, "That's up to you, like I said, I'm good with secrets". Elizabeth takes the hint, smiles at him then extends her hand out to stroke the insides of his thighs. Phil returns the smile as he watches her slowly undo his belt then undo the buttons on his jeans. Phils smile turns into a Cheshire cat grin as he leans back, watching Elizabeth slide off the sofa and onto her knees to fully thank him for staying silent on the matter.

The next day, some of the ladies are in town together having lunch. Judith, Kirsty, Katie, and Claire have gone to visit Tom and Tyler at one of their eateries. Tom has come over to join them to give them some good news. "Hey girls! How's everyone?" he asks them collectively.

All of them reply kindly and ask how he is too. "So...ladies, Tyler and I have some exciting news!". The ladies all coo over in anticipation to what he has to say. "As you know Tyler and I are engaged, and we've kept this bit quiet, but this week we have formally been approved to adopt a child!". "Oh my God that's fantastic news!" declares Judith, instantly getting up to hug him. They all stand up to hug and congratulate him in celebration. "This calls for a celebration!" Claire announces, calling over the assistant to ask her to bring out a bottle of champagne. They all share out the glasses and share a toast with Tom, who asks his assistant to take a picture of them all together celebrating. Nicole walks in and comes over to join them when she spots the ladies celebrating. "Hello, my lovelies, what's going on?". The ladies tell her the good news as she sits down to join them and orders another bottle of champagne to keep the celebrations going. Nicole then sends a group text to Maddie, Indya, Rebecca, Lynda, Clio, and Elizabeth to come and join them.

An hour passes and the ladies are by now well on the way with the drinks and celebrations as the other ladies join them one by one, to form one big group of ladies. Maddie arrives first, who greets them all one by one. Indya and Rebecca turn up next with a card and a gift to give to Tom. Lynda arrives next, bringing balloons that she purchased en route. Finally, Clio and Elizabeth arrive together. As they both walk in, before they get to the table, Elizabeth whispers to Clio, "James is not home later if you are free?", to which Clio replies coyly, "Maybe, I need to see what the home situation is first with the children". Elizabeth smiles as she turns her attention towards the now large group of friends, greeting them all one by one. Everyone seems to be friendly enough towards each other, except Rebecca, who is frosty towards Elizabeth. She is civil enough but Elizabeth can see that Rebecca is not impressed to see her there.

After a while Nicole gets up to leave as she has work commitments to take care of at her Botox clinic.

Maddie announces that she needs to leave too as she has a booking at Nicole's clinic, so they say their goodbyes and together.

As the other ladies chatter half-drunk amongst themselves, Clio gets up to go to the bar. As she waits for her drinks, Elizabeth appears beside her and asks, "So, are you free later?".

Clio smiles back and tells her, "You are a bad influence you do know that?". Elizabeth smiles back and replies, "Life is short, sometimes too short, so you might as well have as much fun as you can". Clio looks at her and pauses for a moment before saying, "How about tonight? Harry is at home and has got a couple of the men coming over for a poker night". Elizabeth smirks and replies, "Perfect, Shall I pick you up?". Clio asks, how much have you had to drink though? Elizabeth tells her, "Don't worry, we can get a taxi". Clio looks puzzled and asks, "A taxi? To where?". Elizabeth chuckles and tells Clio that she has booked a hotel room, just out of town, that they can go to. Clio smiles and replies that she will be ready. "Well, I didn't think that those two would end up being good friends" states Claire, looking over at Elizabeth and Clio drinking and laughing at the bar. "Nor did I, especially as Clio likes to be top dog!" replies Kirsty, who cackles at her own comment, which in turn makes the other ladies begin to giggle.

The afternoon concludes as all the friends part ways and head back to their homes and back to whatever plans they have for the evening. Elizabeth and Clio though, as we know, have quite different plans.

The evening arrives as Elizabeth says goodbye to Harry as her taxi arrives. Elizabeth meets her outside. Both ladies dressed to kill, get in and head off to their planned destination. "So where are we going?" Clio asks Elizabeth. "It's a surprise" Elizabeth tells her, with a smile on her face as she looks at Clio, with lust in her eyes.

As the taxi pulls up, both ladies exit the taxi and head inside the hotel.

"Why don't you go to the bar, and I'll get us checked in" Elizabeth tells her.

Clio smiles, looks at her and curls an eyebrow to accept the instruction, enough to show that she will do as she is told, which she is not used to, as she is usually the dominant character amongst their group of friends, but for some reason she finds Elizabeth intoxicating and unable to resist or to say no to.

Elizabeth joins Clio at the bar as they make small talk and sip their cocktails.

As they do so, Elizabeth is busy on her phone, texting and replying to someone unknown to Elizabeth. The ladies finish their cocktails, then Elizabeth orders two bottles of champagne to take up with them to their room.

Upon entering the room, the ladies begin to embrace and undress each other slowly. After a couple of minutes, Elizabeth steps back and from her purse she pulls out a small bag of white looking powder. "How about a little livener to get the party going?" she tells Clio, who in turn looks at her and smiles broadly. Both ladies take some out and make their lines on the counter, sniffing them up as they play music on the TV in their room and continue to sip champagne.

Elizabeth then begins to fondle and grope Clio as she continues to kiss her neck and body.

Suddenly she stops and pulls out some silk scarves and a blindfold. Clio becomes curious as to what Elizabeth has in store. Elizabeth tells her,

"Put this on" referring to the blindfold. Clio does as instructed whilst Elizabeth kisses her some more. "Now, lie back and spread your arms and legs".

Clio smiles as she does as she is told. Elizbeth ties her up to the corner posts of the bed and continues to kiss and stroke her body.

"Now, the best part" Elizabeth declares. Clio feels Elizabeth climbing off the bed, then moving around the room, wondering what is going on.

She hears the door open followed by Elizabeth muttering something, not loud enough to hear what was said though.

She hears the door shut and begins to wonder what's going on. "Are you still there?!" she calls out.
Elizabeth replies sultrily, "I am still here". Clio smiles as she relaxes, feeling the effects of the alcohol and cocaine running around her body. Clio suddenly feels Elizabeth climb back next to her on the bed and her hands stroking her body.
Suddenly, she feels another pair of hands touching her, strong her body too. Clio suddenly becomes a little anxious, wondering who the hell that is. Then, she feels another pair of hands on another part of her body. By now she is anxious as to what is going on, what is happening, and who the hell the other two people are. Elizabeth chuckles and reassures Clio, saying, "Relax! This is our treat for the night!".
Clio wonders who the other two people are. She still feels a little nervous, especially as she never planned for this, nor can she see who it is. It only takes a moment longer though to realise that it is two men that have joined the two ladies in the room, quickly deduced by the fact that what was put into each of Clio's hands. Whilst Clio nervously begins to pleasure both men with either hand, she feels Elizabeth's hands over her. Clio begins to relax and get into the swing of things as Elizabeth starts to talk dirty to her and the two men.
Finally, Elizabeth unties Clios hands and feet to allow to move more freely. Clio continues to pleasure the men as they move themselves into position to fulfil Clio's fantasies that she has spoken of before to Elizabeth on a previous encounter. Not for one minute though did she ever think that she would carry them out, but then again, Elizbeth is no ordinary woman. Finally, once in the throes of passion and ecstasy, Elizabeth pulls off the blindfold that covers Clio's eyes. Whilst Clio pleasures one of the men she looks up just enough to see that she does not recognise him, something she is quite happy about.
She looks behind her to, to see that she doesn't recognise that man either.

Elizabeth smiles broadly as she climbs off the bed to pour more champagne into their glasses and puts more cocaine on the counter to sniff, whilst Clio is joined at either end by the two men.

Then, what Clio doesn't see is that Elizabeth has slyly picked up her phone, flicked the side switch onto silent, and has begun to take a few pictures, whilst the unaware Clio continues to indulge. After the evening has finished, the two men leave, whilst the two ladies shower then get dressed. Clio, feeling a little embarrassed, asks Elizabeth, "Why didn't you tell me about what was going to happen? What if I said no or something worse?". Elizabeth holds her and pulls her close to stroke her back, replying, "Well then it wouldn't have been a surprise, would it? Plus, this was your fantasy, and why go through your life not having fulfilled your fantasies? Think about it, you didn't do it with Harry and a friend of his so no awkward feelings or emotions to deal with after, the ideal scenario, don't you think?".

Clio thinks for a moment and nods her head in agreement. "Fair enough, good point". By now Clio is gaining her confidence back and begins to become the equal in character to Elizabeth again, to which Elizabeth allows. But she knows how and when to pull the strings, and when to let others think that they are in control.

The taxi arrives as Elizabeth and Clio climb in to go back to their homes. On arrival, they say their goodbyes as they quickly hug outside. "Hi darling, how was your night?" Harry asks Clio as she walks in. Some of the other men smile and greet her as they continue to play cards. "It was good fun actually, rather surprising" she replies to him. As Clio walks off to the kitchen, Harry watches her. In his mind he is hoping that Elizabeth hasn't mentioned anything about them and what they have got up to, but he senses no such thing from Clio, who he knows, if she did, things would have blown up by now.

Two days later, Rebecca is at home. She keeps thinking of her meeting with Elizabeth, distracted by the pictures on her late husband's phone.

She finally snaps and leaves her house angrily, ready for a confrontation. She knocks on the door but is greeted by James. She asks for Elizabeth, but James politely tells Rebecca that she is not home, that she has in fact gone to visit a family member in Hampshire for a few days. Rebecca, not wanting to cause a scene to James, thanks him and leaves. Whilst she walks back home, she calls Elizabeth but no answer. She then sends a text message to Elizabeth, stating that she has decided to contact the police to deal with the matter further, as she now suspects foul play, her message reading, *"Elizabeth. I have decided to take matters further. I am not comfortable knowing that you have been involved with two men and now they are dead"*.

The two blue ticks appear on her screen to show that Elizabeth has read the messages, but still Elizabeth doesn't reply. As Rebecca enters her home, she closes the door and calls the number for the local police station. "Inspector Matthews please" she asks. As she waits, she can feel a small breeze, and upon investigating, she finds the window in one of her rooms downstairs is ajar slightly. Not thinking much else of it, she closes it and returns to her hallway. "Matthews here" comes the voice on the other end of the phone. "Hi, it's me Rebecca, Sebastian's widow. Listen, I want to report some new information towards my husband's murder...". On the other end of Rebecca's phone, Matthews waits for her to finish her sentence, but she doesn't. Finally, he talks back, asking, "Hello? Rebecca? Are you there?" but he doesn't hear anything. In the police station, Matthews is at his desk with his phone in his hand, still trying to see if Rebecca is there. The line goes dead on him. "Carter?" he calls out over the room. "Sir?" she replies. "Grab your coat, we're going out. I just had a call from Rebecca, Sebastian's widow. Something doesn't seem right as she was talking one minute then the line went dead". Carter replies, "Did you try calling her back?". Matthews nods and replies, "I did, but it keeps ringing. If it went straight to answerphone, I'd assume her battery had died, but it hasn't". Carter tells him, "Best to check on her, just in case".

Matthews and Carter arrive outside Rebecca's house and pull up on the driveway. As they exit the car, he tries again to call her on her mobile. No answer.

"Is that her car sir?" Carter asks him. Matthews checks the registration and confirms it is. "Well, she must either be home or has gone somewhere by foot, maybe gone for a run?" Carter assumes. Matthews thinks for a moment then replies, "Well, if she did, then why did the line go dead? Something doesn't add up". Carter nods to agree then knocks on the door and tries the doorbell, to no answer to either method. Matthews tries to call Rebecca's phone again, then, as he listens carefully, he can hear it ringing, just the other side of the front door. Carter looks at Matthews oddly then she puts her ear to the door.

"Erm, some people don't like that kind of thing!" comes a voice from end of the drive. Matthews turns around to see Geoff and Claire, walking with Josh and Judith, smiling back at him with humorous expressions. Matthews smiles as Carter doesn't change expression. "Matthews greets them all then addresses Josh, "Hey, have you heard from Rebecca recently?". "No, why?" he replies. Matthews doesn't answer as he continues to let Rebecca's phone ring. Carter by now is looking through the letterbox. "SIR! She's on the floor, unresponsive" Carter calls out. Everyone rushes over to hammer on the door to get a response. Carter looks through again to declare that she can see a pool of blood on the floor. Instinctively, all of them start to kick and barge at the front door. It begins to loosen and then finally it crashes open. Matthews and Carter rush in to attend to the unconscious Rebecca. Geoff calls for an ambulance as Carter calls it in on her police radio. "Oh my God, is she OK?" Claire asks desperately, as Judith begins to sob in Josh's arms, looking on anxiously. Matthews puts his ear to Rebecca's mouth then puts one hand on her wrist and his other hand on her neck to check her pulse. He then looks up at Carter then at the friends to declare, "She's gone".

July:
Don't Leave Me High

"Sir, the pathology report is back" exclaims Carter to Matthews. "Thank you. Have you read it?" he asks back. "Yes" she replies to Matthews. "And? What do you think?" he asks Carter.
Her reply is, "In a nutshell, she died of her injuries falling down the stairs. Water was found near the top step and a glass tumbler, suggesting that she accidentally dropped or knocked it over, spilt the water, and slipped then fell. She has multiple injuries but most notably the trauma to her head caused a large haemorrhage".
Matthews thinks for a moment, pondering the words, before saying, "Was the tumbler broken?". Carter replies, "There's no mention of it being broken, just that it was found at the top". Matthews thinks for a moment again then asks, "What step was found to be wet?". Carter scans the report briefly to find it, before answering, "The second from top". Matthews thinks again, thumb on his chin, a finger to his lips, his eyes moving left and right through concentration. Finally, he gets up to look at a picture of Rebecca on his office wall, then finally he declares to Carter, "I know Rebecca quite well from dealing with her at the hospital and having been friends with her for some years. She was a very clean and tidy person, very careful about what she does, not one to absent-mindedly leave cups on stairs, of all places. The cup wasn't broken so I doubt it wasn't kicked or dropped as it didn't break. The water just so happened to be right near the top too…". Carter responds with, "Sir, on the other hand it could just have been an accident, they do happen, and she was still grieving the loss of her husband". Matthews looks at her, pausing for a moment, then replies candidly, "I don't believe this was an accident".

The first weekend of July. Most of the friends are preparing for another event. Some have signed up to take part in the town's triathlon.
Some have signed up to help volunteer.

Josh, along with Judith, Andrew, Katie, Geoff, Claire, Tom, and Tyler, are having dinner, having helped Josh and his company to prepare the event for the following day. As the friends enjoy their food and a few drinks to unwind and relax, some of theirs ping with messages in the large group they are in. "Dominic said he will help out tomorrow" Tyler says to the group, reading the message. Josh smiles, unlocking his phone to reply to Dominic to say thank you. Josh messages the group to see if anyone else can help. Elizabeth messages to say that she will, especially as James will be working, being a Sunday of course. Nicole replies to send her apologies, saying that she has too much work to catch up on, stating some payment issue to her employees at the clinic, but wishes good luck to everyone. Maddie replies too, saying she cannot as she has a big account to work on as part of an investment coming up. Josh replies to them with thumbs up emojis. "Have you tried Steve and Kirsty?" Geoff asks Josh. "No point, they never help, even though they have nothing else to do with their time". Judith cuts in with, well, we don't know what people get up to in their time though do we? They might be busy". Josh smiles at Judith, not bothering to argue. Tyler and Andrew look at Josh to offer silent support, knowing that not everyone in their circle is as helpful as others.

The next day, the triathlon is about to begin. Josh addresses the volunteers, assigning them their positions to double check they understand what to do and what to expect. Josh hands over the marshal maps and instructions to several of his friends helping. Speaking to them as a group he says, "Elizabeth, please take Andrew to his spot then you and Dominic are at your spot". Elizabeth smiles sweetly and replies not a problem, as they turn and head off. As they approach the car, Andrew glances at the number plate. He suddenly thinks to himself that he knows he has seen those plates somewhere before, as he thinks long and hard about it.
"Nice car Elizabeth" Andrew tells her.

"Thank you, it's very handy but quite bulky for some of the narrow country lanes sometimes, especially when it comes to parking, I am terrible at that" she replies, smiling as she drives. Andrew chuckles to her response, making light of the situation. She drops him off then heads to her spot with Dominic. The event starts as all the participants make their way through the various stages of the course. Phil messages Maddie to check up on her, asking how she is getting on with work. She replies she is snowed under and will catch up with him later. Elizabeth and Dominic clap and cheer as participants make their way past them. "How's the wife?" Elizabeth asks him. "Oh, she's fine, she's busy today catching up on her business" he replies. "Ah I see, so I have you all to myself then!" she counters back, giving him a knowing smile. Dominic looks at her and smiles, replying, "So it seems!". Elizabeth turns to face the oncoming participants again, who cycle past at various speeds, then turning back to look at him with a glint in her eyes, she says, "You know, we are all alone out here in the countryside. I have a big car too you know!". Dominic looks at her with a smile, "So you do!". Elizabeth chuckles back as she adds, "You know, that day in the hotel, it was rather fun. I think we owe it to ourselves to have a repeat performance…don't you?". Dominic looks at her smiling, nodding in agreement. Dominic messages Andrew to ask if he can get a lift back from his spot as Elizabeth is having a car issue. Andrew replies that he will do so.

"It looks like the coast is clear then!" Dominic tells Elizabeth quite candidly, "Perhaps you should climb inside if you need to remove your knickers!". She smiles at him and chuckles, telling him, "What knickers?" as she raises an eyebrow to his suggestion. Dominic's face grins with delight as they both climb into the car, knowing that they are in the middle of nowhere and can see for miles if anyone were to drive down the road. In the middle of Dominic and Elizabeth engaging in adulterous copulation, his phone rings. He climbs off Elizabeth as he ushers her to be silent whilst he answers. "Darling it's me" comes the voice on the other end. It is Nicole.

"I'm going to be busy throughout the afternoon so once you've finished helping with the event, why don't you go down and join the others" she tells him. Elizabeth can overhear the conversation, and upon hearing going down, she mouths silently to him, "That's a good idea" as she slides down into the footwell of the passenger seat and begins to pleasure him. "Darling...are you there?" Nicole asks him as he struggles to concentrate. "Sorry, yes, yes that's fine, I'll do that" comes his reply, as Elizabeth distracts him. Dominic hangs up and puts his phone to one side as Elizabeth comes back up to resume their activities. "The coast is clear; we have the afternoon to ourselves" says Nicole. "Well don't just stand there, come back and join me under the covers" replies Maddie, throwing back the covers of the hotel bed she is in, revealing that she is naked. Nicole smiles and slides into bed, joining Maddie in a passionate clinch as they begin to fumble under the covers together.

The day arrives for the funeral of Rebecca.
All the friends prepare themselves at their homes as they get ready to say goodbye again to someone close to them. "I still can't believe that she gone" says Judith to Josh. "I know, it's mental, three people we know in the space of six months. I'm half scared to go out now!" he replies, trying to lighten the mood, to which it does make Judith smile.
Josh and Judith drive to the church, picking up Andrew and Katie along the way. Geoff and Claire get a taxi, as does Steve and Kirsty. Tom and Tyler are nearby so decided to walk. Dominic and Nicole share a taxi with Phil and Maddie. Harry and Clio pick up John and Lynda. Elizabeth picks up Indya, Enrique's widow.
The reverend, James, delivers an emotional service as the family and friends listen to the readings and join in with the hymns.
As the service finishes, James goes to the main doors of the church to comfort Rebecca's family as they thank him for a beautiful service. Once the formalities have been concluded, everyone heads to the wake, being held at Redcoats Farmhouse just outside Hitchin.

Rebecca's family mingle and speak to many of her friends from the group that live in Hitchin. Elizabeth goes to the bar, shortly followed by Harry, as they wait to be served for drinks. "Hello stranger" Harry says to her. Elizabeth turns and smiles as she looks at him, replying, "Hello tiger! How are you? Can I buy you a drink?". As the two converse, Clio watches over from afar, looking at Elizabeth, admiring how well turned out she always looks. Maddie comes over to join Clio and teasingly asks, "Worried about your Harry chatting to Elizabeth?". Clio turns to her, thinking that she is not, as she is having lustful thoughts about Elizabeth. "Haha no, I am just waiting for my drink, just seeing how long it is taking" Clio replies. Nicole comes over to join the two ladies, giving them both a gentle hug, more so with Maddie though, based on recent revelations of them being revealed to be having an affair together.

Meanwhile, the men are huddled together as they chat about recent events and life in general. As they talk, Andrew beckons Josh to speak to him privately. "Mate, remember when I said that I thought I'd seen Elizabeth's car before?". Josh recalls the conversation as he nods. Andrew continues, "Well, Katie and I were at the usual club the other night and I saw her car there! It was definitely her car!". Josh begins to chuckle between the two as he asks, "Are you sure?".

Andrew giggles back as he replies, "Yes! 100% it's hers. She gave me a lift at the triathlon event, and I noticed her number plate and car of course. I thought I recognised her car before, but at the club the other night, I saw it again!". Josh by now begins to giggle more with Andrew as he asks him, "Did you see her there?". Andrew smirks but shakes his head and says, "No, but that's the weird thing, I know the club well and there's only so many rooms and public spaces to go, so if she is going, she did well to not be seen, besides, I wasn't looking specifically for her as it wasn't until I went outside afterwards that I saw her car. But it is her car". The two friends laugh together as they watch Elizabeth at the bar, talking to Harry, as they both think, if only the others knew what she is getting up to. Trouble is, some of them do!

Meanwhile, Judith, Kirsty, Katie, Claire, and Lynda, are talking to each other as the reverend James walks over to them. He has changed out of his usual attire when working but has ditched the robes for more casual trousers and a crisp white shirt. The ladies stare at him as he strolls over, admiring his arms and chest and flat stomach, all of them noticing that under his robes he actually has a toned, athletic body.

"That was a lovely service you did today James" Judith tells him. "Thank you, Judith, I hope that Rebecca got the send off she deserved" as he smiles and thanks her. Kirsty, not one to want to miss out on anything, sidles up to him, invading his personal space and strokes his arm to thank him too, then stating, "Ooh, hello muscles! You kept those hidden all this time!" as she outrageously flirts with him. James gently laughs as he thanks her for the compliment and says that not all men of the cloth are old out of shape men or women. Katie also joins in the conversation to him with, "Elizabeth is a lucky lady it seems!" giving him a wink as the ladies' chortle. James smiles and laughs with them as he nods in appreciation of the comments.

Back at the bar, Harry leans in to whisper to Elizabeth, "Fancy being a bit naughty?". She turns to reply, "Here? Now? Where?". Harry diverts his eyes in the direction of the toilets. "Classy!" she tells him as he chuckles. "Meet me in one of the cubicles in two minutes?" he asks. She nods at him and smiles carefully, doing her best to not make it obvious to others. As Harry walks off, Clio walks over to join her. Looking quite serious, Clio says, "Hey, I've been watching you!". Elizabeth looks at her, a little caught by surprise but keeps her composure just enough to ask "Why?" as she smiles at her. Clio breaks into a smile and says, "Because I was just thinking that I want to drag you off somewhere for a quick bit of satisfaction!". Elizabeth smiles broadly at her and says that she would like that too. Clio replies, "I'll meet you in one of the cubicles in a couple of minutes" then seductively licks her top lip in suggestion at what she wants then turns quickly to find a vacant cubicle.

Elizabeth stops smiling as she quicky thinks on how she is going to do this. She loves the idea of fooling around but with both Clio and Harry, husband, and wife, both unsuspecting of each other's recent adulterous history with Elizabeth, at the same time separately. She thinks and thinks quickly at how she is going to do this. She is about to back out on them both, but the idea of this scenario is beginning to turn her on as she works out the logistics. Elizabeth enters the cubicle that Harry is in since he is looking out through the door slightly. "Come on, let's be quick!". Elizabeth declares straight away to him, "We don't have time for sex, pull your trousers down and I will treat you!". Harrys eyes light up as he does as he is told and pulls them down quickly, as Elizabeth quickly goes to work on him, all the while thinking how she is going to see Clio at the same time. An idea enters her head as she continues her activity with Harry, quickly stopping to look up and say, "My phone! I think I left it at the bar, stay there, I'll be back in a couple of minutes!". Before Harry can answer she gets up and exits the cubicle, kissing him quickly, and taking his hand and putting down below on himself, saying, "Keep yourself busy for me!" then shutting the door quickly. She makes her way to the ladies' section of the toilet area, and finds Clio waiting inside a cubicle, her head looking out for Elizabeth. "We must be quick. Sit down now!" she commands Clio. Clio chuckles as she replies, "I love it when you are demanding!". Elizabeth smiles but acts quickly, pushing Clio to the toilet seat as she drops to her knees and pushes Clio's thighs apart as she quickly begins to pleasure her. Clio pushes her hands to the sides of the cubicle as she begins to softly moan. After about a minute of action, Elizabeth suddenly declares, "My phone! I think I left it at the bar, stay there, I'll be back in a couple of minutes!". Surprised, and before Clio can respond properly, Elizabeth puts Clio's hand down below and says, "Keep yourself busy for me!", as she quickly exits the cubicle. Elizabeth rushes carefully back to the cubicle with Harry in it and knocks, announces it's her, and enters.

Before Harry can say anything, she drops down again to continue where she left off, making sure that she uses all her skills and knowledge to bring Harry to a happy ending in double quick time. No sooner than he does, Elizabeth quickly stands up and says she will leave him to clean himself up as she checks the coast is clear, before exiting to leave him to it. She quickly heads back to the cubicle with Clio, knocks, announces its her, and enters. Clio goes to kiss her, but Elizabeth says, "No time for that!", knowing that they don't have time, but also for other reasons that she doesn't think Clio might appreciate. After literally a couple of minutes, Elizabeth has brought Clio to her happy place.

Whilst she recovers, Elizabeth quickly stands up and tells her that she will exit first to make sure no one can see or become suspicious. Elizabeth checks outside the door then exits to head back to the bar and reception area of the wake. About a minute later, Harry walks out from his cubicle and into the shared corridor that divides the ladies' cubicles. As he does so, Clio walks out at the same time. They both look at each other in surprise, both pausing for a moment, wondering if one or the other had heard or seen, but as we know, both are in the dark as to what they have done behind the other ones back. "Hi darling, fancy seeing you here!" Harry tells her, a little flustered, feeling a little sheepish. Clio too is blushing slightly as she greets him with a kiss. "Hello! What are you doing here?" she asks him, pretending to make a joke of being at the toilets at the same time.

They walk out together holding hands, smiling, but not talking. They see their friends and mingle with them in the small groups that have formed, as Elizabeth looks over at them.

First, Harry looks at her and winks, then as she turns to look at Clio, she too winks at Elizabeth. Elizabeth smiles back them both in turns, making sure to not get caught out, then she turns to the bar and lets out a sigh in relief. She calls the barman over and declares, "I think I need a large gin please!"

One week later, the local Titmore music festival is about to begin. Many of the friends prepare by packing their camping gear and bags plus some shopping to take with them, to make the short journey just outside of Hitchin. Upon arrival, Josh and Judith head to their pitch and begin setting up their family sized tent, alongside Andrew and Katie's tent, with Geoff and Claire next to them, creating a mini communal area in the middle for them all to put their chairs up and congregate around whilst they open their bottles of champagne and other assorted drinks and snacks. The men head inside one of the tents to roll a large joint as they laugh and joke, getting into the festival spirit, whilst the wives catch up on the recent activities from their lives.

Phil and Maddie, along with Dominic and Nicole turn up and spot the other friends who are already set up and decide to pitch their tents along with them so that they can all form a larger camping community.

Once completed and all the friends have celebrated the start of the weekend with a few drinks, they head off to the main arena to watch their preferred bands play. As they do they spot some of the others mulling around the VIP area. Amongst them is Harry and Clio, Steve and Kirsty, John, and Lynda, plus Indya too. Josh and the others head over to all mingle and catch up as they drink and listen to the bands play.

After a couple of hours, Maddie announces that she is going back to the tent to get some more cans of G & T. Nicole says, "I'll come with you, I fancy the same too" as she joins Maddie on the walk back to the tents. Ten minutes after that, Josh, Andrew, and Geoff are giggling together as they decide that they quite fancy a little livener, deciding to also head back to the tents. As they do, the next act comes on stage, prompting the other friends in the VIP area to rush out to head to the arena.

Josh, Andrew, and Geoff are still talking away as they approach the camping area. "Maddie and Nicole are taking a while, aren't they?" Josh tells the others, as they nod in agreement.

In the camping area it is busy but not packed, as people are scattered around it, sitting, drinking, and talking, as people's voices carry over the area, coupled with the sounds of the band onstage. As Geoff and Andrew go into Geoff's tent to set up a few lines, Josh manages to pick out low, muffled sounds, coming from Maddie's tent. Curious, he wonders if she might be ill, maybe thinking she has had too much too soon, showing concern, he heads over to her tent and pulls the zip up, and asking at the same time, "Maddie, is that you? Are you OK?".

As he pulls open the flaps, there on top of the mattresses, he sees Maddie and Nicole, together, semi naked, their mouths locked passionately kissing, their shorts around their ankles, as they pleasure each other using their hands. Josh's eyes light up in amazement as the two ladies suddenly stop what they are doing to look up and see Josh in the tent doorway. Instantly they become aghast at being caught. In a split second they stop what they are doing and quickly pull up their shorts, not knowing what to say, where to look, or how to respond. "Oh! Sorry! I'll come back later!" Josh declares to them, as he begins to pull the zip down to afford them some privacy, but not before catching their eye and smiling broadly at them, having witnessed what they were doing.

As he turns to walk away the tent zip opens and Nicole rushes out quickly to grab Josh by the arm to speak to him. She says, "Oh my God, Josh, please don't say anything to anyone!". Josh looks at her and replies, "Look, it's your business, plus I don't gossip unlike others, but if this comes out, I didn't see anything, how's that?". Nicole lets out a big sigh of relief and tells him, "Thank you, I promise". Josh smiles at her as he tells her that it might be a good idea for her and Maddie to make their way back as others will wonder where they are, to which she nods in agreement. Josh heads back to Geoff's tent and joins them, smiling to himself at what he saw. "What's up with you, something tickled you to make you smile?" Geoff asks him. Josh say, "Oh nothing, just overheard something funny from some other campers" as he joins in the class A action.

The following day, everyone begins to wake up from the night before, slightly hungover. One by one the husbands and wives come outside and join in for a cooked breakfast being made by Josh using the camping stoves, and a tea or coffee, brewing away on the camping kettle, all being made by Josh and Andrew.
"Morning mate, how was your night? Did you sleep well?" Josh asks a bleary-eyed Andrew as he emerges from his tent. Andrew smiles back and greets his friends and replies that it was quite good. Katie emerges from the tent next who gives out a big yawn and a stretch as she greets the others. Surprisingly from their tent also emerges a woman they haven't seen before, who goes over and hugs Katie and Andrew and says goodbye, thanks them for a fun night, then disappears across the camp site, assuming back to her own tent. Josh looks and Andrew and Katie and begins to laugh, addressing them both, "Outstanding, even at a music festival you still manage to hook up!" as they laugh back with him. "Did you even get her name?" he asks them, chuckling away to himself. "I want to say Laura, or Lara?" Katie replies with a wry smile. Andrew just shrugs his shoulders and smiles as he passes over two mugs to Josh to fill with coffee.

As the friends sit and chat, Geoff looks over and says, "Is that the reverend James and Elizabeth walking over?". The friends turn and see that they are indeed coming towards them, with a quad bike driving slowly behind them filled with their camping equipment.
"Hello, you two" Josh calls out as they arrive at their area. "Good morning to you all" replies James, smiling as he greets each person. The friends get up to greet both James and Elizabeth and invite them to join for a coffee and breakfast. "That's very kind of you" Elizabeth replies, smiling as she sets up a chair and places it between the wives. As they all sit and talk amongst themselves, Harry, John, Dominic, Steve, and Phil wander over and spot the reverend and Elizabeth plus the others. Elizabeth, spotting the men that she has slept with, smiles sweetly as she says hello to them all.

Harry plays it cool with his greeting, maybe feeling a little uneasy that she has turned up and is amongst the other friends. Phil spots this though and smirks to himself. The men are quickly joined by the other wives who all come over to greet everyone. Each one who has had extra-marital adventures with each other, tries their best to not let on or be over friendly. Judith, none the wiser though, engages in conversation with Elizabeth and asks quite innocently, "How have you been anyway? Have you been up to much recently?". Elizabeth smiles and, whilst not making direct eye contact, she does turn her head subtly in the direction of Harry, Phil, Steve, and Dominic, replying, "Oh you know me, I do like to keep busy with things" as Judith smiles and nods along as they continue their conversation.

As the music begins on the main stage in the afternoon, all the friends get up and head off to join the packed crowds. Some of them head to the VIP area whilst others head to the main standing areas to dance and sing along. Josh, Geoff, and Andrew find a quiet place away from others to indulge in some class A action, all the time laughing and joking. Meanwhile though, in the packed crowded main area near the stage, Elizabeth is gently swaying to the music as she stands with most of the other wives. Her phone vibrates in her pocket with a message.

Steve – "I'm not a big fan of this band. Fancy going to the woods to see the other band that's on?"

Elizabeth smiles to herself as she puts the phone away and continues to dance. After a minute she quietly slips away, getting her phone out and replying to Steve.

Elizabeth – "See you there in 5 minutes".

Steve makes his way over to the woods and finds a quiet area away from the crowd. Elizabeth arrives and looks around, then makes her way over to him. "Hello!" Steve says. "Hi Steve, not a fan of the other band then?".

Steve replies, "They're OK, but I thought it might be nice to catch up with you as I haven't really had a chance to do so since we last met". She turns to look at him and smiles. She knows what he means, but she will play along. "Do you mean when we last shagged? Is that it?" she replies, giving him a knowing look. "Well, I wasn't going to say that! But... yeah!" comes his reply. "Doesn't your wife Kirsty do much to satisfy you these days?" she asks him, catching him off guard. Steve smiles back as he replies, "Well, she's quite boring in bed to be honest. But you, that was something else!".

"You know, James is not back at the camp site. I have an empty tent. Maybe you'd like to carry on this conversation back there?" she tells him. Steve smiles broadly as he nods and replies, "That would be a good idea". With that, they leave and head back to the campsite, trying to make it look like they left separately, making sure that none of their friends are watching them leave, to not arouse suspicion. The trouble is, someone did see them, and someone followed them.

As the friends enjoy the music, a friend of Josh's spots him and comes bounding over. "Hey there sailor!" cried out his friend Ross in excitement. "Ah Ross! Where have you been these last few months? I haven't seen you in ages!". Ross hugs his friend before replying, "Oh you know me! I've been finishing my third degree. I am sooo glad to be done. No more Ruskin visits, all done!". Josh congratulates his friend as they swap recent stories about their lives. "Sooo, have you got any fit single men friends then?!" Ross asks him. Josh laughs and replies, "Not to my knowledge, I think they are all taken!". Ross tuts before adding, "Well, can't blame a guy for trying. Anyway, I'm on the hunt to powder my nose!". Josh giggles, then tells him, "Come with me, I've got a film case in my pocket we can use to key some off from". Ross squeals with delight as they find a quiet spot to partake in some cocaine. As they begin to key the coke and laugh together, Josh spots Elizabeth walking towards the campsite, then, Steve only meters behind.

This makes Josh think, pondering about what they are up to. As Josh and Ross continue to key the cocaine, Josh tells him, "Mate, wait here, I'll be back in a couple of minutes, promise". Ross nods as he smiles and closes his eyes, feeling the effects of the drug, whilst swaying gently to the music playing. Josh begins to walk back to the campsite, keeping his distance but close enough to see what is going on. To Josh's surprise, he sees Elizabeth enter her tent, then after twenty seconds, a shifty looking Steve stops outside it, looks around again, then enters too. Josh creeps over slowly so he is not heard, but he needn't worry, the music is loud enough, and other people are in the site talking and laughing. Josh creeps over to Elizabeth's tent and finds a gap in one of its plastic windows. His jaw drops amazed at what he is seeing. On the floor on her back is Elizabeth. On top of her is Steve, trousers around his ankles, grunting and groaning, as Elizabeth pulls him in tight as possible. Josh watches for a minute, still amazed at what is going on, but at the same transfixed, maybe even a little turned on, as a wry smile appears on his face. Steve doesn't last long though, as his grunts and groans become louder before he lets out one final grunt and collapses on top of her. Josh does his best to stifle his giggles as he tiptoes away from the tent and back to where his friend Ross is.

"What took you so long? Come on, get the coke out!" Ross demands in a playful manner. Josh laughs as he produces the goods as they continue where they left off. As they do, Josh spots Elizabeth walking back to the main arena, with Steve further back. Josh smiles to himself but at the same time, disappointed about what his friend has got up to. "Hey Steve!" Josh calls out. Steve glances around and spots Josh and Ross in a small indent in the trees and bushes and walks over, looking around all the time. "Hey! What are you guys up to then?" Steve says tongue in cheek, seeing clearly what they are doing. "Where were you earlier? I was looking around for you to come and join us" Josh tells Steve, pretending to sound innocent. Steve hesitates before replying, "Oh that. I had to go and relieve myself". Josh smiles, thinking, I bet you did.

August:
It Helps to Have a Dog

"Morning Sir, here's your coffee" Carter tells Matthews, passing some much-needed caffeine. "Thanks Carter. How was your weekend?" he asks her. "Good thanks sir, not too busy luckily" she replies. Carter smiles at her before turning his attention back to the PC screen. "What are you looking at on there?" she asks quizzically. Mathews pauses for a moment to reply as he breaks his concentration away from the screen to face her. "I've been thinking about the local deaths that have taken place since the start of the year. Three deaths. All part of a circle of friends" he states, stroking his chin in thought. "Do you think they are related somehow?" Carter asks him. Mathews says, "The evidence we have suggests not, based on how they died. Two of them were mugged it seems, and the other is down as accidental death...". "But...?" Carter replies, expecting one. "But... three deaths, three people part of the same circle of friends, plus I think Rebecca's death still has unanswered questions". Carter nods to agree with him. "I think we should carry on digging for more evidence for all of them" he tells her. "Forensics have done everything they can though haven't they?" she asks. Matthews nods then adds, "Yes, they have done what they can, but I feel that we should do some more research ourselves. Maybe more CCTV footage from wider areas that we haven't seen yet. More visits to that click of friends too". Carter nods to agree as she sits at her desk, clicking away on her PC to find more CCTV footage as Matthews begins to do background checks on the group of friends.

Meanwhile, Tom and Tyler are at the end of an interview. "So, we have finished our background checks on your both. All the paperwork has been completed and verified by our team". Tom and Tyler sit side by side in the interview, both looking anxiously at their interviewer. "So, what happens now?" Tom asks nervously. Tyler grips Toms hand, waiting for the verdict on their outcome.

"I am delighted to announce that your application to adopt has been approved. All you have to do now is wait until someone suitable becomes available, based on everything that we have gone through. When we have a list of candidates, we will be in contact to show you and invite you in when you have made your choice".

Tom and Tyler let out huge sighs of relief, then turn to hug each other, the emotion of the situation getting to them as they both shed tears of relief and joy. The interviewer smiles broadly at them, telling them, "You are going to make wonderful parents, congratulations" as she stands up to shake their hands. Tom and Tyler both shake her hand and thank her, even going in for hugs as they bean with happiness. Tom then gets his phone out to text the group of friends. Almost straight away, messages start coming back, with everyone congratulating them both on their achievement. The messages from everyone also state that they should all go out tonight to celebrate together, to which Tom and Tyler agree.

That night, at one of Tom and Tyler's restaurants, all the friends gather at a large table, as food and drinks are brought to them, with champagne bottle corks popping, the guests laughing and joking with each other. A happy scene to witness from the outside. On the inside, various persons give each other subtle glances, suggestive glances, especially those that have had interactions with each other. The men are all smartly dressed in their various attire, mostly jeans, shirts, and jackets on. The women are dressed smartly too, some quite daring, one or two quite provocatively. Elizabeth being one of them of course.

As Elizabeth gets up to head to the toilets upstairs, Phil gets up moments after her, as the others continue to talk amongst themselves, not paying much attention nor suspecting either, why would they?

As Phil is first to emerge, he waits outside in the corridor and pretends to be on his phone, waiting for Elizabeth to emerge. When she does, she greets him. "Hello Phil!" she says, giving him a smile, eyes fixed on his.

"Oh, hello!" he replies, pretending to look surprised to bump into her. "So, how has your week been?" She asks him politely, all the while looking at him with a smile. "Good thanks and you?" comes his reply. "Slow, but today's news has been good to hear, it's lovely to come out and celebrate". Phil nods his head in agreement. "I suppose we better get back or people might talk!" she says suggestively. Phil sees that as his cue to carry the conversation on further. "There's nothing for them to talk about, we haven't done anything!" he replies, looking at her suggestively. "No, we haven't, not tonight anyway" she replies, now with a smile on her face to suggest that maybe another encounter could be on the cards. Phil hears the words, thinks, then quickly replies, "Maybe another night then" he says, not as a question, more of a remark or suggestion. She stops and turns to look at him, flashing him a smile, then replies, "What's wrong with tonight?". Phil quickly becomes quite aroused at the thought, watching her as she begins to walk away, but as she does, she stops for a moment, then lifts her skirt up just enough to reveal that she is wearing black lace top stockings and suspenders underneath her figure-hugging dress. "Text me later, yes?" she tells him. "I'm sure you can find an excuse to find some time". Phil smiles back at her, doing his best to conceal his obvious excitement. Elizabeth looks down at his waist, below his belt, seeing his excitement. "Might be best to tuck that way when you come back in, but not so much later though" she tells him, letting her dress fall back down to its original length again. Phil laughs as he makes much needed adjustments to his trousers, taking her advice. "See you back at the table" she tells him, smiling at him seductively as she walks away, heading down the stairs. Phil waits for about a minute before heading back down too, joining his friends. "You were gone ages, what were you up to?" asks his wife Maddie. "Oh, I bumped into a friend, and we got chatting" he replies, smiling at her, then kissing her cheek. As she smiles and turns away to talk to the others, he notices Elizabeth looking at him, with a wry smile on her face, followed by a gentle wink to let him know what is on the menu later. Phil smiles back as he thinks about how he can make it work to meet up with her.

As the evening concludes, the friends begin to leave one by one. Some of them are quite drunk, especially some of the wives, as they cackle and struggle to talk to each other. One by one they climb into their taxis to take them home, with most of them all on the same road, Knights Road. Phil makes it his priority to make sure that He and Maddie share a taxi with Elizabeth and James. The reverend sits in the front as he talks to the taxi driver, whilst Phil sits in the middle between Elizabeth and Maddie. It is obvious that Maddie has had quite a lot to drink and is slurring her words. Elizabeth talks to Maddie as Maddie rests her head on the window and head rest, giggling and slurring, but whilst she does so, Elizabeth slips her hand into Phils trousers and begins to reignite his excitement. "Would you both like to come back to ours for a nightcap?" Elizabeth asks Phil and Maddie. Phil looks at Elizabeth, knowing full well what she means, then asks Maddie, "What do you think Maddie?". "Yay! Let's party!" she replies drunkenly. "It that OK with you darling?" Elizabeth says to James. He turns his head to look at her, smiling, "Yes of course". Elizabeth then glances at Phil as she smiles at him, as she continues to stroke him down below.

The taxi pulls up and all four get out and head indoors to James and Elizabeth home. They all head to the main living room as James fixes drinks for them. After about ten minutes of chatting, Maddie passes out from the drinking, gently snoring. James fetches a blanket for her and puts it over her, then announces that he too is going to bed. "My apologies, but I have a very early start tomorrow, long journey ahead!". Phil asks if he and Maddie should go. James replies, "Oh, no! stay and have some fun, don't let my departure stop the party! Besides, Maddie looks quite comfortable where she is!". James kisses Elizabeth on the cheek as he heads upstairs and away from the others. Phil turns his attentions back to Elizabeth, looking at her, admiring her.

She looks back at him, then over to the sleeping Maddie, then back at Phil, then nods her head to the side, suggesting they head off into one of the other rooms in the house. Phil gets up and follows her to the smaller living room, more cosy, less informal looking, like a snug. Phil goes to shut the door, but Elizabeth pulls it slightly open again. "Just in case!" she tells him, referring to if Maddie suddenly woke up. "We can see and hear if anyone is coming" she tells him. Phil smiles and replies with a raised eyebrow, "Hopefully the only two people doing that will be us". Elizabeth smiles and lets out a small chuckle as she lies back into a sofa, looking at Phil as he stands by the door. She begins to hitch her skirt up, showing him her stocking clad thighs, using her hands to put on a show for him. Phil watches on, mesmerised, his eyes fixed on what she is doing to herself. She stops, gets up, walks over to Phil, and begins to kiss his neck, using her hand to pleasure him. Phil hears a noise from downstairs and tries to see what it is, but Elizabeth says, "Don't worry, everyone is asleep, that's just the water pipes in the house" assuring him and using her other hand to tun his head back to face her, as she locks lips with him. Elizabeth then drops to her knees and pulls trousers down and begins to pleasure him with her mouth. Again, Phil hears a noise, this time making it out to be Maddie making a brief moaning noise. He is about to stop but again Elizabeth says, "Don't worry, she is extremely drunk, we all make silly noises when passed out!". Phil smiles and nods at her, as Elizabeth then lowers her head again to continue. After a couple of minutes, Elizabeth stands up, kisses Phil on the lips then declares, "My turn" as she steps back, lies on the sofa and parts her thighs for him. Phil smiles with delight as he gets on his knees and repays the compliments given to him, as Elizabeth closes her eyes, mouth open, her hand on Phil's head to pull him in. Once she has reached her desired outcome, she tells him to get on top. Phil obeys and climbs on top of her as she lets out a quiet moan of pleasure. The night it seems, for Phil and Elizabeth, finished with quite a bang.

The next morning, Maddie wakes up and sees Phil next to her on the sofa, sleeping. She wakes him up and says, "God I have such a hangover". Phil laughs and asks if he can do anything to relieve it. "No, its fine, I'll take some pain killers when we get home, all of a few houses down the road!" she chuckles, before holding her head in hangover pain. As they get up and walk out the door Phil asks her, "As we are not doing anything today, shall we cosy up in bed?" making it sound suggestive of what he would like them both to do, clearly still turned on by what happened with Elizabeth last night. "Sorry darling, I am too hungover for any of that today, besides, it feels like you had your fun with me last night!". Phil laughs then says, "Darling you fell asleep as soon as we got there, we certainly didn't get up to anything". Maddie smiles through the pain and replies, "Well it feels like you did!". The couple open their front door and head inside their home.

Later that day, Maddie looks at her phone to see several missed calls from Nicole. Maddie calls her back straight away, as she walks into another room away from Phil. "Hi, how are you?" Maddie asks Nicole, whilst holding a glass of water with more pain killers fizzing inside it. "Well, it's nice of you to finally reply. I'm fine thanks, just wondering why you have been ignoring my calls" Nicole tells her down the phone. "Oh God sorry, my phone was on silent" as she switches it back to normal. "That's not good enough Maddie, I've been waiting all morning for you to turn up, you could have told me". It dawns quickly on Maddie that her and Nicole had planned a morning out together, with a hotel room booked out to so that they could spend some intimate time together. "Just so you know, you can pay for the bloody room. I'm going home, I am so angry right now" then she hangs up abruptly. Maddie holds her head again as she tries to call her back, but clearly Nicole is in no mood to talk to her, ignoring her calls. Maddie sends a text to apologise again, seeing that Nicole has read it, but still no reply.

As she tries to call Nicole again, she feels nauseas and runs to the bathroom, and as Nicole's answerphone beeps for her to leave a message, she begins to vomit, glass in one hand, phone in the other, not her best look one might suggest!

The next morning, Kirsty is in the gym doing her work out when Nicole shows up. "Oh hey, how are you?" Kirsty asks her. Nicole replies with a smile, "Hey! Good thanks, how are you?" as Kirsty replies that all is well. "Just trying to lose some additional timber" Kirsty tells her, sweating away as she works out on the cross trainer, dressed in a baggy t-shirt and tracksuit bottoms. "Don't be silly you look lovely!" she replies to Kirsty, putting her hand on Kirsty's arm to reassure her. "Thanks, but I am not blind and so is no one else! And you can you work out over there too you skinny bitch! You are putting me to shame!" Kirsty tells her jokingly, referring to Nicole's toned frame, clearly on display in her small tight black shorts and tight black vest, clearly happy with how she looks and not afraid to show it. Nicole laughs at Kirsty's comment and climbs on board the cross trainer next to her as the two ladies catch up on gossip.
Once the ladies have finished their workout they head into the changing rooms. Nicole puts on a bikini top and bottoms as Kirsty puts on a black bathing suit, then they head to the sauna for five minutes, then into the steam room as they continue to talk, sitting side by side so that they can see each other as it is full of steam, and they cannot see more than a meter past their own eyes. As they do so, Nicole pays Kirsty a compliment, telling her, "I know you may say otherwise but I think you have a beautiful body, trust me, you look lovely". Kirsty smiles at her and thanks her for the compliment, smiling and chuckling, but adds, "Tell that to Steve! Sometimes it feels like he's not interested in me in that way". Nicole smiles back and says, "Well then he is clearly blind!".

Kirsty smiles back at Nicole, as they both look at each other, maybe a bit longer than normal, before turning their heads away to look forwards, with Kirsty feeling butterflies in her stomach. The machine hisses as it lets out more steam, filling the room up even more, to the point where the two friends even struggle to see each other. Kirsty breaks the silence and says to Nicole, "Do you think Steve doesn't fancy me anymore, is that why he doesn't seem interested in my physically anymore?". Nicole turns to Kirsty and says with a smile, "Don't say silly things! If I was a man, if I was Steve, I would be all over you!". Kirsty laughs then kisses Nicole on the cheek tenderly and says, "Thank you". Nicole smiles back as she kisses Kirsty back on her cheek and replies, "You are welcome, and I mean it too". The two ladies then fix eyes on each other, smiling in appreciation, then Nicole, with Maddie in her thoughts and thinking to herself that she wants to get back at her for letting her down, leans in quickly to kiss Kirsty on the lips, holding their kiss for a few seconds. This catches Kirsty by surprise, as her eyes widen with shock. Nicole quickly pulls away and apologies to her, but then Kirsty leans in to kiss her back, this time, with both ladies locked in a passionate kiss, as their hands come up to hold each other's faces, as they embrace. After a few moments of kissing, Kirsty pulls away and says, "I think its time I had a shower". Nicole looks at her, smiling but with a hint of disappointment on her face.

As the steam room door opens, Kirsty turns and says to Nicole, "Aren't you coming with me?". Nicole looks at her, as a knowing smile comes over Kirsty's face, that makes Nicole smile too and stand up, leaving the steam room. As the door shuts, a hand inside the steam room wipes away the condensation and a shocked face appears, looking through the glass door, watching Kirsty and Nicole walk away. It is Judith.

Judith exits the steam room and heads to the showers, her mind wondering what on earth is going on. As she silently heads into the shower area, she can make out two bodies pressed close together, both in the same cubicle. Only the sounds of running water conceal the noise of them kissing.

That evening, as Steve and Kirsty make dinner and drink wine, Steve innocently remarks, "How was the gym today?". Kirsty blushes but plays it down saying, "Oh it was good, nice workout". Steve continues, "I spoke to a mate earlier who goes, he said he saw you in there with Nicole". Steve's comment was innocent, but Kirsty reads it wrong and thinks that Steve has been told what she and Nicole might have got up to and decides to confess. "Oh, Steve look, it was only a quick kiss, more like what girly friends do, that's all". Steve looks surprised and follows it up with, "Kiss, what kiss? What are you on about?" but by now, Kirsty has said too much as he looks at Kirsty, waiting for her to explain. "Yesterday I was talking to Nicole about something that made me a little upset and she consoled me, then we ended up sharing a kiss". Steve pauses to think and take in what she has said. "What was so upsetting that you and Nicole had to kiss?!" he asks her. "Because, well, I was telling her that our sex life has been a bit stop start recently, and she put an arm around me and then we ended up sharing a kiss. I am so sorry. Nothing else happened I promise". Steve goes quiet as he thinks about what she has said. Kirsty looks at him, her eyes suggesting she is sorry about it. She finally breaks the silence with, "Please say something". Steve looks at her and walks over to where she stands. Kirsty prepares herself for an almighty argument, but instead, Steve grabs hold of her and pulls her close to him, then begins to passionately kiss her, as she responds back to embrace with him. As they get caught up in the throes of a passionate kiss, Steve begins to pull at her clothing to undress her, as she hurriedly pulls down his trousers, revealing that he is hugely aroused by what they are doing. Steve quickly turns her around to push her upper body over the counter and connects with her, as the pair lock in passion. Kirsty, whilst caught up in the excitement, begins to talk dirty to Steve, thinking to herself that what she has said has clearly turned him on, telling him if he liked the idea of her kissing another woman. Steve grunts and groans back that the does, as the pair continue their encounter by the worktop. As Steve continues behind her,

Kirsty says to him, "Would you like to see me kissing another woman?". Steve grunts back that he would. This is now giving Steve ideas about setting up an encounter and the chance for him to push for a threesome with him, Kirsty, and another lady, making him come to a happy conclusion with their activity. Steve thinks, and hopes, that the other person could be Nicole, as she is clearly an attractive lady, but he is happy for another woman to share a night with him and Kirsty. Once they have concluded and dressed, Kirsty asks him, "Please don't mention any of this to Dominic or Nicole, or anyone for that matter". Steve replies, "Absolutely, no way, let's keep it between us". If Steve wants to instigate a threesome with another lady, he knows it's best to follow Kirsty's advice.

That weekend, Josh, Judith, Geoff, Claire, Andrew, and Katie head off on holiday for a few days away to relax in the sun.
Whilst they are outside on the first day, all drinking, they are catching up on what they have all been up to. As they all swap stories, Judith jumps in with, "Oh my God! I have one to tell you! I was at the gym this week and after my swim I went in the steam room, and I heard two women talking then they started kissing!". The others laugh as they ask her for more details. "But that's not the best part! That part is that I know who the two women are!". The others look at her and ask for more details on how she knows them. "Judith replies, "Because, the two women are our friends!". The friends all display shocked looks on their faces before quickly pressing her to reveal who. "I heard Nicole and Kirsty talking, then I heard kissing sounds, then, when they left the room, I looked through the steam room door and saw that it was in fact them!". The friends begin to giggle and comment as Judith continues, "I then followed them to the showers and saw that they were sharing the same cubicle and were quite clearly pressed up close to each other!". Goeff replies, "Amazing! But how did they not see you in the steam room?".

Judith replies, "Trust me, that room is full of steam and sometimes you struggle to see your own hand if you held it out in front of you, but it doesn't hide voices or sounds!". The friends begin to reply and talk about how or why it happened. Katie asks, "So how the hell did it happen?". Judith then tells them about the conversation between Kirsty and Nicole in the steam room and that Kirsty was moaning about her sex life with Steve, and then she assumes Nicole must have consoled her. Andrew laughs and adds, "Sounds like she consoled her a bit too much!" to which the friends laugh. Katie adds, "God! I never thought I'd put those two down as having a bit of a wild side, especially with another woman!". Josh smirks as he says, "Well, you know what they say, there's nowt queer as folk!" making the group of friends burst out laughing. Once they settle down, Josh decides to add in what he saw at the music festival. "Well, it might be Kirsty's first same sex kiss, but it isn't Nicole's". The group turn to look at him, waiting for him to add more to his comment. Judith asks him, "What do you mean?". Josh replies, "Well, I'm not supposed to say as I promised them, but I saw Nicole and Maddie in the tent at the music festival getting, how you might say, quite cosy". Judith looks at Josh and enquires, "What do you mean you saw them in the tent? Where you in there with them too?!". Josh replies, "No of course not! But when I went back to the tents to get some Colombian marching powder, I heard muffled noises from Maddie's tent so I unzipped the front and asked if she was OK, only to be greeted by the sight of them both, shall we say, indulging each other". Geoff and Andrew straight away pipe up with, "Oh my God, was that when we all went back for a sniff?". Josh laughs as he nods his head. Whilst the others giggle away and talk about the two situations, Judith gives Josh a bit of an awkward look. Josh whispers to her, "What? It's not like I did anything! I didn't exactly hang around to watch the show or anything!" Jesus!". Judith thought doesn't seem impressed and replies, "Why did you tell me this earlier? I'm your bloody wife for God's sake".

Josh replies, looking quite annoyed, "Look, they were quite upset at being caught and begged me to promise not to tell anyone, which I think to my credit, shows that I can keep a bloody secret if people ask me to! It's not like I've hidden someone's mastermind crime, is it?!". Judith knows that he is right, but she still thinks, and tells him that he should have told her at least. "Well, you kept your little bit of knowledge quiet until tonight, didn't you? It works both ways darling!" finishing with a slight amount of smugness in his look. He knows he is right, and what annoys Judith is that she knows he is too. She half-heartedly scoffs at him then turns to join in the conversations with the rest of the group.

The following week, everyone is back in sunny Hitchin and making their own plans for the week and weekend ahead. It's a Thursday night and Nicole has arranged to meet up with Kirsty at Santorini's. prior to the arrangement, Maddie has been in contact with Nicole to ask about meeting up, but Nicole has replied that she has plans that night so she cannot meet her. Maddie asks Nicole if they are OK, to which Nicole replies that they are but her text reply still comes across as a little short, not her usual style of texting, to which Maddie picks up on. Maddie decides to give some space to Nicole and sends a smiley emoji then leaves it, leaving Nicole to calm down more, and decides to make her own plans to go out Phil. The problem is, they too are going to Santorini's on the same night as Nicole and Kirsty.

When Maddie arrives with Phil, they find a table and sit down and chat as drinks are brought over to them. Phil's phone rings so he answers. Whilst he is talking, Maddie turns her head around the club behind her just to see who is there and to generally browse, people watch as it were. To her surprise, she spots Nicole at a table across the club, and sitting with her is Kirsty. Maddie smiles to herself, pleased to see her two friends and gets up, but before she is about to walk over, she spots under the table that Nicole has her hand on Kirsty's leg and is stroking it, as the two women chat quite close up to each other.

Maddie stops in her tracks and thinks for a moment on what to do, then decides to walk over to them. "Oh, hi Maddie!" Kirsty says, a smile appearing on her face as she greets Maddie. Nicole looks up and smiles, greeting Maddie too. Both Nicole and Maddie know that their secret is not public knowledge, especially as they both have husbands, and Maddie assumes that Kirsty is unaware too, so she keeps her cool and sits down next to them. Maddie puts on a front as she makes conversation with them, all the while though giving Nicole certain looks to suggest she has seen something, making Nicole ponder about what Maddie might know. After a couple of minutes, Maddie gets up, making her excuses to leave as she states she is out with Phil for the night. As she walks away, she instantly pulls her phone out and sends a text to Nicole, telling her exactly what she saw just a couple of minutes ago. Nicole hears her phone beep, opens it to look at the message sent from Maddie, then turns around to see Maddie, sitting at her table and looking back at her, a surprised look. As the two ladies look at each other across the club, Nicole now feels a little sheepish, whilst Maddie has the look of a woman scorned.

The next morning, Phil heads off to work as Maddie works on her laptop dealing with her financial investments. She is on the phone to a client when the doorbell rings. She opens the door and to her surprise, Nicole is there, half smiling, with a small gift in her hand, asking if she can come in. Maddie lets her in as the atmosphere is a little frosty.
"Drink?" Maddie asks her, keeping the tone cool. "Yes please, thank you" comes Nicole's reply. "So, what brings you here?" Maddie asks her. "I wanted to say sorry for what happened last night and for the way I have treated you". Maddie looks at her blankly and replies, "And what way was that?". Nicole changes her mood slightly into one of frustration as she counters, "Oh come on Maddie, please don't be like that, after all we've been through, it was just a silly mistake". Maddie looks away as she listens, annoyed at having to listen.

Nicole gets up and moves over to Maddie to put her arms on her waist but Maddie recoils slightly. "Please, I'm sorry" Nicole continues, trying to get Maddie to look at her. "Did you sleep with her?" Maddie asks. "Oh, come on Maddie, none of this situation makes for simplicity. We are both married women for God's sake and we are having an affair with each other! What part of this is all normal?". Maddie softens as she knows Nicole is right. Maddie looks at her and says, "Maybe so, but that's not the real point, is it? It feels like you had gone out of your way to make a point after our argument, and not exactly the best way to do it was it?". Nicole looks at her and nods her head in agreement, "Can we put that behind us though and move on? I've missed your company". By now, Nicole is moving closer to Maddie, her arms around her waist, gently pulling her towards her own body. Maddie has the look of resignation and admits inside her own mind that she has missed Nicole's company, especially the physical element. Nicole then gambles and moves in for a kiss, her lips contacting Maddie's for a few seconds. At first, Maddie pulls away gently, then she looks at Nicole and moves back in, both passionately kissing. After a minute of kissing and stroking, Nicole suggests that they go upstairs to which Maddie breaks into a smile and nods along, as Nicole takes her hand to lead her into the main bedroom.

A couple of days later. Clio is at home by herself as she relaxes on her sofa as her cleaner is busy at work in her home. Her phone vibrates with a message. It is Elizabeth. "What are you doing tonight? X" it reads. Clio perks up as she thinks for a moment, knowing that she doesn't have plans, so she replies, "Nothing planned x". Clio waits with a little excitement, knowing that her past encounters with Elizabeth have not exactly been tame encounters. "Want some fun later? I have a little adventure planned". By now Clio is starting to smile to herself as she wonders what Elizabeth might be scheming. "Sounds like fun!" Clio replies in her message.

She waits for what feels like ages, then finally her phone vibrates again as the reply from Elizabeth reads, "Dress as sexy as you can x" followed by a picture of Elizabeth wearing a black basque, fishnet stockings and suspenders and black heels. The picture makes Clio smile broadly as she studies the picture, becoming aroused. She looks around to make sure that the cleaner is not near her, then parting her thighs slightly and takes a picture to send back in reply, also writing, "Does it involve this? X". Elizabeth replies with a heart emoji, followed by, "Meet me outside at 9pm x".

The day passes slowly for Clio as she does her routines and family business but making sure to text Harry to let him know that she is going out tonight. Harry replies that's fine and asks who with, so she thinks of a friend's name to say she is going to catch up with that he has heard of, but someone that he wouldn't think to contact to check up on. Harry gives the thumbs up emoji to her message, making Clio smile, as she then prepares for the night out with Elizabeth, still not knowing what she has planned.

The evening arrives and Clio dresses up as requested but making sure to not overdress to make it obvious to Harry. As she waits patiently, her phone pings to show a message from Elizabeth to come and meet her outside and to walk up the road, away from their neighbour's and friends who might potentially spot them. She says goodbye to Harry then exits her home, then she walks up the road as instructed, to see a car parked up and waiting, engine running. As she approaches it she sees Elizabeth get out from the backsets to greet her. Elizabeth beckons her to get inside the car as she looks around to make sure that no one spotted them. As Clio climbs in she can see that someone is in the driver's seat but cannot make out who it is, as she nudges Elizabeth to silently ask who it is. Elizabeth smiles at her and shakes her head as if to suggest that she won't say but that all is well and to not worry. The car pulls away, heading to an unknown destination as far as Clio is concerned.

"So, where are we going?" Clio asks Elizabeth. She turns to look at Clio and smiles and simply replies, "It's a surprise!".
After about 20 minutes of driving, the car pulls up and Elizabeth opens the door to climb out, followed by Clio, who looks around to check her surroundings.
"Where exactly are we?!" she exclaims, looking around half excited, half nervous at the same time. Elizabeth looks at her and simply replies, "Watch and you'll see!" with a devilish smile and look in her eye. Clio looks around to see that they are in a car park in a small, secluded woods. No one else seems to be around, only the headlights of the car that they arrived in. Elizabeth walks away from the car and stands about five meters away then stops. She removes her flimsy coat to reveal a tight figure-hugging black dress, complete with her stocking on and calf length black boots. Clio watches on, puzzled, only to be startled as several car head lights suddenly switch on, all pointing to where Elizabeth stands. Clio is totally puzzled as to what is going on, then, the penny drops. Several car doors open, followed by the sounds of footsteps on the ground. Clio watches on amazed as she sees the shadows of the people emerge into the headlights, reveling them to be men, all walking and surrounding Elizabeth. Clio watches on, mouth open, stunned by what she is seeing, as Elizabeth slowly drops to her knees and begins to massage two of the men through their jeans, who standing closest to her. Elizabeth takes one more look at Clio and gives her a wink, before she removes the trousers of the first man and begins to pleasure him, as the hands of the other men begin to stroke and fondle her, with her dress being pulled up to her waist as one of the men stands behind her, then he too dropping to his knees to get behind her to return the pleasure in her direction.
A million thoughts run through Clio's head. She feels totally out of her comfort zone and contemplates turning back to get in the car, but at the same time she is mesmerised by what she is watching. As she stares at the action, she too feels a pair of hands on her and decides that she too will succumb to the desires of the situation.

September:
The More the Merrier

September. A new month on. All the friends prepare their respective families for the new terms ahead. Summer holidays have now been concluded, but in Hitchin, it's business as usual.

Things had begun to quieten down but as with this group of friends, things soon pick up again.
Phil is in the local coffee shop, working on his laptop, when Harry walks in and sees him. They greet each other and once Harry has bought this coffee, he takes a seat next to Phil as they begin to talk about life and work.
A message flashes up on Harry's phone, something that Phil spots, knowing that Harry too has seen Phil notice it. Harry at first looks a little sheepish as Phil grins broadly at him then remarks, "Aren't you going to reply?". Harry half smiles as he picks up his phone and is about to see what Elizabeth has written. Quite obviously it is a text asking if he is about and wants to come over for some fun. "What does it say then?" Phil asks, still smiling. Harry, knowing that there's no point trying to hide it, begins to relax a bit as he reads it out to Phil. Both men sit in silence for a moment smiling, then Phil asks him, "So, what's the reply going to be?". Harry thinks for a moment, not sure what to say or write, but Phil interjects with, "Tell you what, write that you are on your way and that you have a surprise for her". Harry looks at Phil a little confused and asks him what he means. Phil smirks and replies, "Mate, you're not the only person that she fools around with you know!". Harry thinks for a moment before realising that Phil must be talking about himself. "You?!" Harry asks him. Phil smiles and gives him a nod. "And I bet we're not the only ones" Phil counters. Harry thinks then nods in agreement. "So, what do you suggest?" Harry asks him. Phil looks at Harry, picks up his coat and says, "Come on, let's go have some fun with her!". Harry shakes his head chuckling as they both get up to leave. "No touching each other!" Harry tells him, laughing. Phil laughs back, saying, "Nope!"

Elizabeths phone vibrates as she opens it up to see that Harry has replied. Elizabeth's eyes light up when she reds it, as she walks up her stairs slowly to her bedroom, opening a drawer to pull out her black basque and stockings. After dressing herself up, or down if you like, she pus on a pair of black stilettos and walks downstairs in a see-through negligée, waiting for Harry's arrival. Elizabeth makes herself comfortable on the couch with a glass of wine, then the doorbell rings. As she opens the door, she is quite surprised to see Harry standing there, with Phil. "Oh, hello!" she says, looking quite surprised and confused, then giving Harry a funny look to suggest what's going on. Harry and Phil don't say anything, just choosing to smile as they both walk through the door, not exactly giving Elizabeth a chance to ask any further questions. "Expecting company?" Phil asks her, noticing the racy outfit she is wearing, as they make their way to the kitchen. "I thought I was" she replies, a little dejected, thinking that, then she pauses and thinks for a moment about why Phil is there, knowing that she text Harry, who has still turned up. She looks at them both, her mood now lifted slightly and quizzically asks, "So, what do I owe the pleasure of your company today then chaps?" as she looks at them both, trying to read their body language. The men look at each other, smiling at each other then look back at her. She gives them both a funny look, half knowing what they mean, but still waits for more information to be given to her, teasing it out of them almost. "I'm sorry you'll have to tell me more than just a look!" she tells them both. Harry pulls out his phone and replies, whilst looking at her then turning to Phil, saying, "This is the surprise I said I had!". Elizabeth looks at them both, knowing that the truth is now out there for them all. She eyes them up and down, smiling to herself, before replying, "Well, now that you are both here, I think I would like to enjoy my surprise, if you don't mind!". Harry and Phil are now smiling like Cheshire cats, as Elizabeth notices that they are both obviously aroused at the situation they now find themselves in.

"So, what are you both waiting for, are you going to unwrap your surprise then?" as she teases them by parting her negligée enough to reveal her stocking tops. Both men don't waste any time as they walk over to her. Elizabeth puts her drink down as she allows both men to kiss her neck and grope her, their hands wandering over her body to stroke and caress her, whilst removing her negligée to reveal her outfit of choice for the occasion. As the men pay good attention to her body, she takes a gulp of wine as she throws her head back with a big grin on her face, looking up at her camera that is fixed to the corner of the kitchen. "Shall we take this upstairs?" Harry asks her. "Not yet, let's carry on down here for now" she replies, knowing that she her camera is filming them. Elizabeth stops them both briefly from their endeavours to pull out a small bag of cocaine. The men look at her, quite surprised but quite pleased too. She pulls out her credit card to chop up six lines, two each, then proceeds to roll up a fifty-pound note then snorts the first line. She passes it to Harry who does one, then to Phil who does his. "I have an idea boys" she then tells them. Before they can ask what, she slowly pulls down Harry's trousers, then holding him in one hand, she carefully scrapes one line on to his obvious state of arousal. Harry and Phil look at each other, now staring to giggle. Elizabeth carefully then snorts a line from him, then once she gets to the end of the line, she gives Harry a flick of the tongue on the tip of his excitement. Phil, seeing this, wastes no time and removes his trousers as he steps in line for his turn. Elizabeth chuckles as she repeats the same trick on him. The final line is left for the men to share and hoover up.
Elizabeth then seductively licks the countertop, slowly, making sure the men can see, making sure that no powder is left behind, as they watch, excited, grinning.

Elizabeth lies back on the kitchen island, allowing Phil to work his way down her thighs and in between to pay her close attention, whilst her hand encourages his head to do so.

Harry moves himself to where her head is, then removing his trousers, allowing Elizabeth to return the pleasure in his favour.

After a few minutes, Elizabeth stops them both before they get too carried away, telling them, "I think it's time we went upstairs boys, don't you?".

Both men grin at her as they fix themselves by removing their trousers, so they can walk upstairs to her bedroom of choice. As they climb the stairs, Phil reaches out to cup Elizabeths bottom and ask, "So Elizabeth, is there anything that you don't like, in this area?". Elizabeth stops and turns her head around to look at him, with a wry smile and declares, "Nothing is off the table". All this does is excite Phil and Harry even more as they all continue their journey to the bedroom.

The next day, Steve is walking through town, talking on his phone to someone, when he spots Nicole. He hangs up as they greet each other. "So how have you been?" he asks her. She replies that she is fine and is busy with life admin and her clinic, just general chit chat, when Steve changes the subject. "So, I heard about your little gym encounter!" he tells her. Nicole is a taken aback slight by him knowing but tries to play it down. "Oh, that. Its not as bad as it sounds, you know what us girls are like!" she replies, trying to sound cool about it all. "Anyway, she was upset, and she kissed me first!" she tells him, making it sound like it was Kirsty who initiated it. Steve just nods along smiling, knowing that it's a piece of information worth holding on to. Steve then tells her half-jokingly, "Well, the next time you both decide to share a kiss, at least let me watch!". Nicole chuckles as she replies, "Why, do you like watching your wife with someone else then?" she asks him, making it sound like an off the cuff comment. Steve smirks as he replies, "Show me a man who wouldn't like to watch his wife put on a show with another woman!". She smiles and jokes back, "You men are all the same!". Steve laughs and nods his head and shrugs his shoulders to agree. As they continue to talk, it does make Nicole think about what he said, after all, now that he knows, anything is possible.

"Right, I'm on my way home" Steve tells her as he goes to say his goodbyes. "I'm actually going home too; did you drive into town?" she asks him. Steve replies that he walked and would appreciate a lift back. They head to her car that's parked in the Queen Street car park, climb in and head off. As they travel back, Nicole is caught behind a parked bus, so she decides to pull out and speed around it. as she does so, a police car is coming in the other direction, to which she narrowly avoids hitting. The police car instantly does a U-turn and puts its blue lights on behind her. "Oh great, just what I need" she tells Steve tongue in cheek, who in turn looks a little concerned about being pulled over by the police. An officer steps up to Nicole's now open window and begins to talk to her about the maneuver that she just did. As he talks to her the officer notices a small, laminated piece of card, looking like a small envelope, beside her mobile phone in the accessory tray by the gearstick. "Miss, would you mind passing that item to me please?" as he points to the parcel. Nicole suddenly realises what he means, then her face drops, knowing that she is about to be caught driving around with cocaine on her. The officer opens it up to see traces of cocaine inside it, then asks her to step out of the car. Steve too is asked to step out as now both officers from the police car interview them roadside. Nicole admits to the officer what it is and tries to make her excuses about it, saying that it was left there by a friend, and it wasn't hers. The officer doesn't buy it and subsequently carries out a drugs and alcohol test on her roadside. She passes the alcohol test but because she has cocaine, albeit traces, the officer has no choice but to arrest her to take her down to the station to carry out the drugs test. "But this is ridiculous, I've told you what happened!" she protests. "Miss, that may be true, but we cannot take your word for it. We have witnessed a piece of dangerous driving and you have cocaine in your car, so we must take you in for a further test". Nicole is clearly not happy with this as Steve too looks concerned. "You too sir. You will have to come with us" the other officer tells him. Steve tries to protest his innocence but to no avail.

At the station, the drugs and alcohol tests are repeated, showing that Nicole is under the limit for both, clearing her of being under the influence from either product, but is nonetheless charged with possession of a class A drug. Once the formalities have been completed, they are free to leave the station, but the trouble is, as they walk out from the station, they are both spotted by Judith, who was outside at the local shop buying some vapes. They didn't spot her though, as she does her best to conceal herself.

Later that day, Judith does the school run and as always, bumps into Kirsty and Lynda, who do the same run and pick up. Judith takes Kirsty to one side and tells her, "I'm sure this is all innocent, but I saw your Steve and Nicole walking out of the police station earlier". Kirsty is shocked by this is asks, "What do you mean? He hasn't said anything about this to me, are you sure it was him and Nicole?". Judith replies that it definitely was, trying her best to be sympathetic. Judith is not one to stir the pot like others might, but she thought it right to tell her friend. Kirsty thanks her and discreetly moves out of the way from the other parents to call Steve. Judith surreptitiously watches Kirsty on her phone talking to Steve as she engages in conversation with Lynda about other things in life going on. Once Kirsty has finished, they collect their children and begin to walk off. As their children run off ahead and play and walk with other children, Judith and Kirsty engage in conversation about the incident. Kirsty tells Judith. "So, it turns out that Nicole was giving Steve a lift back from town as he bumped into her, and she was pulled over for dangerous driving, and she had a bloody left-over parcel of cocaine in her car!". Judith looks at her shocked, but not overly surprised. "Oh no! So, was that why they were at the station? Were they both arrested or something?". Kirsty nods her head at Judith to agree. "Idiots!" Kirsty states. "Anyway, Steve is fine as it wasn't his or him driving, but Nicole will probably get a fine for her driving and probably a caution or something for possession". The two ladies are nearly home as they part company and say their goodbyes.

Kirsty opens her door to see Steve in the kitchen with a glass of red in his hand. "Nothing to celebrate really is it darling!" she tells him. "I'm not exactly celebrating anything! Just having a glass to wind down from today's lovely experience!" he counters. As Steve tells her about it all, Kirsty's phone rings. It is Nicole. Kirsty looks at it and tell Steve she will take it in the other room, as Steve curiously watches her walk off.
"Hey! I heard all about today's little adventure!" Kirsty tells Nicole over the phone. "Oh, it's nothing, it will all blow over" Nicole tells Kirsty. "More like the blow was all over you!" Kirsty tells Nicole, with both ladies laughing together about it all. "Anyway, besides that, I had a good little chat with your husband today!" Nicole tells Kirsty. "Oh really? what about?" Kirsty replies curiously. "He knows about our little adventure at the gym, and he said that if there's a next time, to at least let him watch!". Kirsty laughs and replies, "Did he now? The dirty little sod! I bet he did! He can mind his own business!" comes her reply to Nicole. "Oh! Well, I was thinking that if there's a next time then why not!? If he knows what happened and, if there is a next time, then why not make his little wish come true!" Nicole remarks, letting the statement linger in the air for Kirsty to consider. "Hmm, maybe, I'll think about it! Kirsty replies, but the tone in her voice suggests that she is probably open to the idea.

The weekend comes and some of the friends have met up to celebrate Geoff's birthday.
Josh, Judith, Andrew, Katie, Claire, and Geoff of course, head over to Redcoats Farmhouse for their pre-booked meal. The champagne is flowing as the six friends engage in conversation about the last few days in their lives and what plans they have coming up.
Josh, Geoff, and Andrew get up to go outside to enjoy a vape and talk about when they will next meet up to go for run together. As they arrive outside in the main yard, they hear music being played from within the function barn. The three friends walk over to take a closer look, the sounds piquing their interest.

As they approach the doors, a couple of guests filter out into the yard, laughing, giggling, clearly intoxicated from the party that they are at. The friends decide to poke their heads in the door to take a closer look, chancing their luck. First, they head to the bar and order a drink to make it look like that they are part of the party, then they head to the doors of the main barn to see what or who the party is for. The friends are quite surprised to see that the party host is none other than Indya, the widow of Enrique. "Well, thanks for the invite!" Geoff sarcastically says to Josh and Andrew, who nod and laugh with him. "All these guests and no invite for us?" Andrew adds. They stand in the doorway watching Indya parade around, lording the adulation from her guests. The room is filled with flowers, balloons and other assorted products that add to the setting to suggest it could be a party for a particular reason. "It's not her birthday, we know that" Josh remarks, before adding, "So what is this party for?!". Geoff and Andrew just shrug their shoulders as they too have no idea, choosing to sip their drinks as they watch the party guests mulling around the complex.

Indya is then joined by a man who wraps his hand around her waist and kisses her on the cheek, in a way that would suggest that they are more than friends.

"Maybe it's HIS birthday!" Geoff remarks, making Josh and Andrew think. Josh looks at a table to his left and sees gifts and cards on it. "Looks like it could well be" he tells his friends. Geoff picks up one of the cards to read to see who the man is. "Christ!" Geoff remarks to his friends with surprise. "What?" Josh and Andrew reply in unison. Geoff passes then the card for them to read.

"To Indya and Pavel. Congratulations on your engagement!" it reads.

"Wow!" Josh replies with surprise. "When did that happen?!". Andrew adds, "So let me get this right, she is now engaged to some random who we have never heard of, and Enrique died in March, and now it's September, and she's engaged?!".

Just then, Josh's phone rings. "Hi, where are you all?!" asks Judith on the other end.

"Just gatecrashing Indya's engagement party!" Josh replies. The natural set of questions quickly follow as the men are soon joined by their wives. As they enter the barn and take in their surroundings and listen to their husbands as they bring them up to date, they are quickly spotted by Indya, well, it wasn't hard for her to miss the group of friends. "Oh hiii!" she exclaims, as if she was greeting her best friends. "How are you all?" she adds. Judith forces a smile and replies, "We are good thanks. We are just next-door having dinner and wondered what all the commotion was". Indya looks at the friends, who on the outside are smiling, but deep down probably feeling a little bit disappointed that they were not invited, especially as they are all friends and neighbours too. Indya then starts to feel a little guilt come over her as she tries to explain her way out of it.

"I'm so sorry that I didn't invite you guys, I really mean it, but it's been such a trying time and I've been caught up in this whirlwind since Enrique died, that Pavel and I met and he has helped me in my grieving process, then things have quickly gone in that direction. Enrique was your friend and I just thought that it would have been a bit awkward". The friends all smile back at her as Katie puts her hand on Indya's arm to suggest that they understand. That is until they spot Steve, Kirsty, Phil, Maddie, John, Lynda, Harry, and Clio all on the dance floor drinking shots.

"Did you have trouble telling them then?" Katie remarks, quickly removing her sympathetic hand from Indya's arm. Indya turns around to see the invited friends all drunkenly dancing, her eyes fixed for a few seconds on them as she watches them having a good time. When she turns her head back around, five out of the six uninvited friends have already walked out, leaving Josh standing there, just looking at her emotionlessly. "I, I don't know what to say" Indya says, looking sheepish and quite foolish. "It's your choice who you invite" Josh replies, then taking a sip of his drink and turning to follow his friends out of the exit.
Indya rushes out to stop him and try to explain but Josh replies, "My meal is getting cold" before walking off.

The next morning Indya messages the scorned ladies one by one to apologise and tries to explain that she feels terrible for not inviting them. Each reply she gets back is the same tone, polite but short.
Later that day, at different times of the day, Judith, Katie, and Claire all find a bunch of flowers on their doorsteps with a card to apologise again. Each lady in turn replies to Indya via text to thank her for the flowers, but again the replies are kept simple, and conversations kept short. This may take some time for their relationships with Indya to heal.

Later that night, Josh receives a text from an unknown sender. He is cautious, wondering if it is a scam text as he doesn't have the number saved in his phone. But he can see that the message is a series of pictures. His curiosity gets the better of him, so he opens it up and clicks the pictures to download them. "Wow!" he says with surprise, then starts to semi laugh at what he has been sent.
"What are you wowing at?" Judith asks him. Josh holds his phone up to show her the pictures. "Wow!" Judith exclaims, joining Josh in his surprise.
On his phone are pictures of Kirsty, with her tongue down the throat of one of Enrique's former teammates, and her hand down his trousers on his groin.
"I don't think she would enjoy knowing that these pictures exist" he tells Judith. "Especially as its clearly not Steve!". Josh agrees and adds, "And I bet that he doesn't want his wife knowing either! Especially as he's got two children too". Judith asks who the footballer is, and Josh tells her, not that she cares much about the sport, nor has she heard of him, but Josh knows very well who the player is. "Who sent them?" she asks him. "No idea, I don't have this number saved" he replies. "Well, probably best to ignore it and don't get involved" she tells him. Just then, Judith's phone pings too, with the same pictures and from the same unknown number. "Oh, well it looks like it isn't going to be a secret for too much longer!" as she opens then up to show Josh. A few minutes later, the micro-chat groups they share with some of their friends is awash with banter.

October:
Trick and Most Definitely a Treat

As the summer months finally disappear and the weather turns colder and the nights start to draw in quicker, there is no let up with all the friends in Hitchin. Parties come and go, birthdays, anniversaries, substance abuse, alcohol flows a plenty, intoxicating affairs, secrets and lies still fill up their calendars.

One lunchtime, Clio has decided that she wants to pay a visit to Elizabeth, so she sends her a text and waits for her reply. Soon enough, Elizabeth texts her back, inviting her to come over. Clio gets herself dressed up and makes the short journey next door. Upon entering, she gives Elizabeth a kiss on the cheek and then one on the lips, to suggest that she would like to play. Elizbeth duly obliges as she gropes Clio's bottom in the process, saying, "Someone has come over feeling quite horny!", to which Clio chuckles and replies, "Well, Harry is out, and I've exhausted Mr. Pink (referring to her favourite toy of pleasure) and I thought to myself we haven't caught up recently". Elizabeth smiles and replies, "Well as you know it's always good to see you" as she passes a glass of win to Clio. As the ladies' chat, Elizabeths phone pings with a message. She looks to see who it is and reads it to herself as Clio continues to sip her wine. Elizabeth smiles to herself as she reads it then puts the phone on the table. "Anything interesting?" Clio asks, wondering what has made Elizabeth smile. "Oh, just someone sending suggestive messages" she replies coyly. "Oh really? And there was me thinking I was the only one!" Clio chuckles back, but inside her head she does wonder who it could be.

The doorbell rings. Elizabeth pauses their conversation as she excuses herself to answer it. Clio continues to sip her wine as her attention turns to whom could be at the door. She can hear a man's voice but cannot make out who it is or why they are there, but Elizabeth seems to be happy and deep in conversation with the visitor.

Clio notices that Elizabeths phone is on the table still. Unlocked.
She thinks for a split second, and her curiosity gets the better of her and picks up the phone and quickly opens WhatsApp to see what her neighbour and part time secret lover gets up to. Clio has known Elizabeth since January, a solid ten months now, and they have shared many evenings together, some clean living, some not so, but what she realises is that does she actually know her deep down? She doesn't know her intimately, well, not in a non-sexual sense anyway! The Elizabeth she sees and speaks to is a well-dressed, extremely attractive lady in public, but a deviant behind closed doors with an insatiable appetite for the taboo. What she didn't expect to see was how close to home Elizabeths games have been.
Clio hears the front door close then watches Elizabeth enter the room again.
As she sits down and picks up her wine to sip, Clio looks at her dead in the eyes and asks, "Elizabeth, can I ask you a personal question?". Elizabeth looks at her body language and senses she is about to ask something serious. "Of course, anything" comes her reply. Clio looks to the side to think how to ask her question and mumbles before Elizabeth interjects with, "Come on Clio, spit it out". Clio's eyes dart back to Elizabeth and quick-wittedly replies, "Is that what you did with Harry's?". Elizabeth laughs at the quip, then after a couple of seconds, realises that Clio is not actually joking. "Clio what's wrong?" Elizabeth asks her, her laughter ending abruptly.
"Elizabeth, please be honest with me, tell me how long you and Harry have been fooling around" comes Clio's response. Elizabeth looks at her, then away slightly, biting her lip, before returning her gaze back at Clio and replies, "I don't know, a number of months, probably just before we started to fool around". Clio, surprisingly, remains calm, taking in the information, almost appreciating the honesty and quickness of the reply. Elizabeth breaks the ice with, "I'm sorry, I know to hear that must be upsetting". Clio looks at her quickly and replies, "If you knew that then why do it?!".

Elizabeth shrugs her shoulders and counters, "Have any of us been angles? Think about it, if it wasn't me, it would have been someone else". Clio counters, "But that's not the point though is it! I know you! You're my bloody friend!". Elizabeth nods and says, "I know, and it's not great I get it, but what we have got up to is just as bad, if not worse! What about the hotel room? And do we start on what happened at the car park that night?!". Clio, a little shaken and annoyed, takes in the reply and her body language softens as she comes to the realisation of the whole situation.

Elizabeth lets out a sigh and replies, "I get that point, but how would Harry feel if he found out we had been sleeping together behind his back?". Clio instantly pipes up, half serious but with a slight joking tone with, "Knowing him he would bloody love it! And knowing him he would bloody want to be part of it!". Elizabeth chuckles as Clio begins to smile back too. "Look, none of us have behaved ourselves" Elizabeth says, adding, "And from today onwards, I won't let it happen again". The room goes silent for a few seconds as Elizabeth looks at Clio, wondering what she is thinking. Clio finally replies, "I don't want you or him sleeping together behind my back… you can do it only when I'm there!". Elizabeth looks at Clio, quite taken aback at her comment, looking at whether she thinks Clio is being serious or not, as Clio sips her wine. "Okaaay then" comes Elizabeth's reply, still wondering if Clio is being serious or not. Clio breaks the silence again with, "Where's James tonight?". Elizabeth replies that he is busy with work. "At the church? I didn't think Clergymen worked so late in the evenings, especially as it's not a Christian occasion" comes Clio's reply. "Busy with other work, don't forget we do have businesses to take care of" comes Elizabeths reply. Clio looks at Elizabeth, silently, letting her eyes do the talking, as she holds her gaze on her, her mouth concealed by the wine glass. Elizabeth can then just about make out the corners of Clio's mouth have an upturn, suggesting a wry smile, then Clio says, "Well don't make plans tonight, we're coming over". Elizabeth looks puzzled and replies, "Who's we?". "Harry and I" Clio says.

Later that day, as afternoon turns to the evening, Harry arrives home. Clio looks at him deadpan, then as he turns to face her, she cracks a small smile. "How was your day dear?" she asks him. "Oh fine, just busy taking care of things" he replies. "I bet" she says under her breath, but now is not the time for that conversation. Right now, Clio wants to have some fun. "Darling, I've arranged for us to have a drink next door shortly". Harry looks at her and replies, "Sure, what time do they want us?". Clio replies, "I think Jaes is busy tonight so we're just having a catch up with Elizabeth". Harry smiles at her as Clio turns to leave the room, saying, "I'm off to get ready". Harry is puzzled then says, "Ready? We're only going next door". Clio pops her head back through the doorway and replies, "Sometimes darling it's nice to dress up and feel good about oneself, don't you think?". Harry smiles and agrees. Clio pops her through the door again and says, "Look sexy for me please darling, I do like to show you off you know" followed by her blowing him a kiss. Harry smiles broadly as he puts his things away and goes upstairs to shower and get ready.

"Hurry up darling, are we not supposed to be there by now?" Harry shouts out to Clio, who is just at that moment walking down the stairs. Clio is dressed in her tightest black, backless minidress, complete with strappy heels and black nylons. Her hair is curly and her make up immaculate. "Wow!" Harry exclaims, "I feel like I should have made more effort, aren't we more dressed up for going to Santorini's or something?" he adds. Clio smiles and replies, "Don't be silly, I felt like dressing up tonight, besides, who knows, we could easily end up going out somewhere after". Clio gives him a kiss as they shut the front door to make the short walk next door, knowing full well that she is trying to throw him off the scent.
"Hello, you two, come on in" Elizabeth says as she opens the door to her home fully for them to walk in. Clio gives her a polite greeting and a kiss on the cheek as she enters first. Harry greets Elizabeth, playing it cool, but he notices that she too is dressed up just as sexily as Clio.

Once inside, Elizabeth offers them a drink, making sure to pour them all a large glass. The three of them make small talk as they in turn talk about their day and week so far. Elizabeth as always makes sure to not let on what the evening is about, nor does Clio, but Harry's eyes wander between the two ladies, unsure as to why they are both dressed up even though that they do not have plans to go out, but then again why would he? He doesn't know that both women are aware of everyone's exploits between each other... not yet anyway.

Elizabeth decides to put some music on and goes to a cabinet in the main living room and produces a large bag of white powder then puts it on the table. "Shall we liven things up a little?" she tells them, rather than asking. Harry and Clio don't need to be asked twice as they start to produce notes and cards to delve into the class A delights on offer by their hostess. AS they begin to chop the powder up and form lines, Elizabeth produces another bottle of champagne, popping the cork and topping up their glasses. Clio notices that Elizabeth has discreetly left a pack of cards on the table too, so picking them up, she takes them out and starts to shuffle them and plays a quick game of blackjack with Harry, whilst Elizabeth potters around downstairs in the kitchen and living room, flitting between the two, being a busy bee doing what ever it is she is doing, or scheming perhaps.
As she settles down on the sofa next to Clio on one sofa and both ladies facing Harry on the other, she says, "Ooh cards, what are you playing?". Harry tells her, although Elizabeth knows anyway, using it as an introduction to her next line of suggestions. "Deal me in on the next game then". The three of them are now playing card games for about ten minutes, with whoever loses having to down two fingers worth of drink, with the winner getting to snort a small line of the Bolivian marching powder before them on the table.
"Right, I think we should up the ante on the games, there's only so much of all that stuff we can handle so quickly!" Elizabeth says to them with a smile.

Clio looks at her, knowing what is to follow, and replies, "I'm game, what do you have in mind?". Harry's demeanour perks up as he listens to what follows. Elizabeth looks at them both and declares, "Whoever loses each hand must remove an item of clothing, how's that then? It's only harmless fun, yes?". Harry clearly loves the idea but looks at Clio to see her reaction, expecting her to turn the idea down, but to his surprise he is greeted by Clio replying, "Ooh that sounds like fun, let's do it! Harry? Are you OK for that?". Harry looks at them both, smiling and nodding, trying to remain cool, but inside his head and elsewhere, a fire has been lit, thinking to himself that this is turning out to be a great evening. He still hasn't clocked on though that it has been planned by both ladies, and the fact that they are dressed up as sexily as can be for just a supposed quiet night in.

A few rounds pass as each person loses a game, removing an item of clothing or an accessory, such as a belt and socks for Harry, earrings, and bracelets for the ladies, then harry loses his jacket, followed by his shirt. Next to lose is Elizabeth, having to remove her dress, revealing her bra, knickers, and stockings and suspenders. When her dress comes off, Clio remarks what a beautiful body she has to her, then asking Harry, "Doesn't she have a beautiful body, Harry?", to which Harry tries to play it cool by murmuring back to Clio that she does. Next to lose is Clio, who stands up to say, "Oh well, rules are rules, my turn!". Clio peels off her dress to reveal that she too is dressed in the same attire as Elizabeth. Both ladies' giggles as they sit side by side on the couch, drinking their champagne, as they watch Harry smiling broadly to himself, trying his best to look at his cards but knowing full well that he is using very chance possible to look at the two semi naked ladies in front of him, dressed in very sexy underwear. Harry is next to lose, having to remove his shirt, then loses again to remove his trousers. For the next round, Elizabeth makes sure that she loses by taking an extra card when she didn't need to. "Oh dear!" she exclaims, standing up to remove her bra.

Harrys eyes scan her body as the item is removed. By now Harry is shuffling uncomfortably in his seat, almost to the point of reaching for a cushion to hide his obvious state of arousal from them.
Next to lose a game is Clio, with it know her turn to lose her bra. Upon removing it and sitting back down again, Elizabeth compliments her on her chest, asking how beautiful they look, to which Clio thanks her and giggles. Harry loses the next game, and having only one item to remove, his underwear, stands up and turns around to hide his modesty, then grabbing a cushion to hide himself as he sits back down. "Oh, someone's being a spoilsport!" Clio says to him, giggling along with Elizabeth. Harry is surprised by her comment, assuming that Clio wouldn't have previously gone even this far.
Next to lose is Clio, who stands up and turns around to face away from them as she begins to remove her knickers. As she does so, she slides them down slowly, sexily, making sure that her bottom is on show to Elizabeth and Harry. As she does so, nearly reaching her ankles, Elizabeth gives her a playful smack on the bottom, saying, "Now that's a thing of beauty right there Clio!", making Clio continue to giggle. As Clio sits back down, and makes a poor attempt to cross her legs, Harry notices that Clio has done some fine manicuring, more so than usual, making him now twig, thinking, "was all of this planned?".
The next game, Elizbeth makes sure that she loses, and upon standing up, turns around to start to remove her knickers, but, as she slips the first part halfway down her waist, she turns around to face them both, before finally removing them. "Oh, Elizabeth, you bad lady!" laughs Clio excitedly. Harrys eyes by now are on stalks as he smiles like a Cheshire cat, watching the ladies giggle, drink and snort the occasional small line in front of them.
Harry loses the next game, but having nothing left to remove, tells them that the game is surely over.
"Not yet it isn't!" Clio remarks to him. "We have items still! It looks like you'll just have to do a dare!". Elizabeth replies to her comment with, "Agreed Clio, you don't get out of it that easily Harry! Come on, stand up and pour us a drink!".

"And without that cushion too!" Clio adds. Harry pauses for a moment, slightly blushing but does as he is told and stands up, removing his cushion to top up their glasses. "Oh my, are you finding this game a little bit of a turn on Harry?" Elizabeth asks him whilst Clio giggles. Harry doesn't reply, as he continues to grin from ear to ear, picking up the bottle to top them up. "It looks like you are ready to hoist up all sails as you are at full mast Harry!" Clio tells him. Harry chuckles as he finishes pouring the drink, then sits down and reaches for the cushion again, only to be told by Elizabeth, "No, no cushion, a bit pointless now don't you think? That ship has sailed!". Harry laughs at her comment and does as he is told.
The next game played; Clio makes sure to lose.
"Oh, damn it, I have nothing left to take off!" she remarks. Harry reminds her that she still has her stockings and suspenders on. "I'm not taking these off, they don't count as clothing" Clio tells him. Elizabeth agrees with, "Mmm hmm, agreed Clio, I'm with you on that one, same here". Harry thinks for a second, then declares, "Well, I had to do a dare, so you'll have to do one too!". By now Harry understands this has all been set up. Why though he doesn't know, especially as he has quite a bit of history with Elizabeth, and behind Clio's back too, but Harry's arrogance and attitude is that he is not ashamed nor cares by this point, not that he will mention any of it to Clio, but he still assumes that Clio doesn't know about his antics with Elizabeth. Both ladies as we know, do. Another aspect is that Harry hasn't even considered how James might feel about the fact that his wife is sitting there practically naked, but all of the above as mentioned, gives him no cause to consider it.
"So, what's my dare then?". Harry's mind has a thousand ideas but chooses to try and play it safe just in case he is wrong and that maybe there is a point that all this will stop. "How about you have to stroke Elizabeths breasts for thirty seconds?". Clio giggles as she looks at Elizabeth, who reclines back slightly on her side of the sofa to stick them upwards a little, whilst smiling broadly.

Clio leans over to play with Elizabeths breasts, using her hands to slowly stroke and tease them with her fingertips. "OK, times up!" Harry announces, sounding half disappointed. As Clio takes her hands away from a smiling Elizabeth, Clio leans forward a little more to use her tongue to give one of her nipples a quick lick, followed by a kiss. Harrys eyes nearly pop out from the stalks they are already on, his face beaming with delight at what his wife has done, thinking to himself that this is out of character for her, but he doesn't care by this point.

The next game played, Elizabeth makes sure that she loses, with Harry playing it safe to make sure that he doesn't have to pick up cards that would make him lose. "Oh dear!" Elizabeth says with alleged disappointment, a total fabrication and with no hint of it in her voice. "Well Harry, what's the dare then?" she asks him. Harry suggests that she should return the favour to Clio, as she had duly obliged.

Elizabeth sits up and leans over to return the compliment to Clio, who leans back, smiling, closing her eyes to enjoy. Harry struggles to keep an eye on the timing of thirty seconds, instead choosing to not even bother. After a minute has passed, Elizabeth asks him, "Surely a minute has passed!". Harry laughs and replies, "Yeah it did, about thirty seconds ago!". Elizabeth gives him a cheeky look but with a glint in her eye.

Another round of cards, which proves to be the final one, but unbeknown to them, is played. Clio loses again. "Oh dear, me again?!" she says, now with no conviction in her voice at allegedly losing. "So, what's the dare Harry?" she asks him. Harry shrugs his shoulders and asks, "I don't know, you tell me!". Clio smiles at him then at Elizabeth as if to ask her what to do. Elizabeth looks at Harry, but her reply is to Clio, "You have to kiss my neck for thirty seconds". Clio's face smiles and shows a willing acceptance of this. As Clio leans in to kiss Elizabeths neck, Harry leans in a little further from his set to watch, and by now he is as excited as can be.

Elizabeth closes her eyes as she leans back to enjoy Clio's lips wander over her neck, but then raises her hands up to take hold of Clio's head and pull it up from her neck and to her face, where both ladies lock lips in an open mouthed long lingering kiss. Harry cannot believe his luck, sitting there, watching two beautiful women, dressed only in lingerie, kissing each other. Harrys desires take an upturn more so too. As the ladies' lock lips in a passionate clinch, Elizabeth moves one hand down to Clio's legs, stroking her thigh, then moves her hand between Clio's legs, to which Clio obliges by parting them widely for Elizabeth to explore between them. Harry by now is transfixed. A tornado and earthquake could hit where they are but it's doubtful that he would even notice.

As Clio enjoys Elizabeths wandering hands, she too moves her hand down between Elizabeths legs to return the favour, with both ladies now stroking and playing with each other.

Clio moves her mouth away from Elizabeths for a moment to ask Harry, "Has thirty seconds gone by?". Harry as quick as a flash, replies, "No, not yet!", knowing that he is fully lying, but both ladies giggle as they too know that thirty seconds had passed by about two minutes ago. "Well, I suppose I still have some more time left then" Clio replies to him, but with her eyes fixed on a smiling Elizabeth. "Maybe I have enough time to do this then" as she stands up, then moves between Elizabeths legs, and gets down on her knees, using both hands to push Elizabeths legs wide apart, to then use her tongue in more ways than one.

Elizabeth sits back and groans with pleasure, moving her hands on to Clio's head to keep it in place. "Aren't you going to join us Harry?" Elizabeth moans at him. Harry stands up and thinks about where to go. Clio, deep in concentration at her task in hand, puts her hand backwards to take hold of Harrys hand and pulls him forwards and ushers him to stand next to where Elizabeth head is. "Take care of him for me, would you?" Clio mumbles. Elizabeth moves her head up just enough to start pleasing him with her mouth.

Harry, right now, is in his element, thinking to himself that it doesn't get any better than the situation he is in now, and he didn't even ask nor sneak around for it to happen. Everyone is in consent of what is going in. He is still of course very much unaware that the ladies know about each other's past, with him, and with others too. For now, they plan to keep it that way, just enjoying the pleasure of the flesh on offer. After a couple of minutes of the activities being carried out, Elizabeth moves her head away and suggest that they should swap over. Clio gets up and takes her seat on the sofa, with Elizabeth getting onto her knees, returning the favour to Clio. Harry moves his waist towards Clio's head, but she instructs him, "No, I want to watch you behind Elizabeth". Harry looks at her with a broad smile on his face, with Clio looking back at him with a devilish look in her eyes. From hearing Clio's instructions, Elizabeth parts her thighs wide, inviting Harry to join with her. Harry pushes the table out of the way, but not before taking one more line from it, then downing the closest glass of champagne to him too, then proceeds to follow his wife's instructions.

A couple of minutes pass as all three writhe and moan from the alleged unexpected turn of events.

Clio suddenly pushes Elizabeths head away and declares, "Now, I'd like to watch you both together whilst I sit and play, then I'll join in!". Elizabeth doesn't need asking twice as she lies on the floor, ready for Harry to move on top of her, to which he doesn't waste much time doing so.

Clio gets up to grab a drink of champagne and indulges in another small line from the table, but as she does so, she takes hold of her phone and making sure that it is on silent, she surreptitiously takes a few pictures of her neighbour and friend, and her husband, indulging in their cavorting activities. "Now, I want to see you both pleasing each other at the same time" she demands. Elizabeth and Harry oblige. Again, Clio secretly snaps a few pictures.

"Shall we take this upstairs? I have a very large bed that is begging to be used" declares Elizabeth after a couple of minutes. Clio smiles widely and stands up, followed by Elizabeth, and of course, a very excited Harry.

The next morning, after the dust has settled from the night before, Clio and Harry wake up in their bed, both with slight hangovers. "Wow, that was an unexpected evening!" Harry tells her. "Was it?" replies Clio. "What, do you mean that you had that planned all along?!" Harry replies to her teasing comment. Clio just looks at him, smiling, then turns over to get her phone. She unlocks it and shows Harry the pictures that she took. "When did you take them?!" he asks her, confused, but quickly realising that it must have been when it was only him and Elizabeth in action. Clio rolls her eyes at his question to suggest that it was obvious when she took them. "Why did you take them?" he asks her, and at the same time, moving his hand towards Clios thighs from under the covers. "Because I wanted a nice reminder of the evening" she tells him. Harry smirks as he tries again to move his hands to Clio's inner thighs, but she keeps them tightly closed, only for her to then say, "Also, it's a nice way for me to see what you have already done with her". Harry looks at her with surprise, trying his best to not know what she meant, by asking, "What? What do you mean?". Clio looks at him, and stays perfectly calm to reply, "I know you have already slept with her Harry, several times too. I saw the messages on her phone when she wasn't looking. I know everything that you have got up to". The colour in Harry's face drains away as he tries to think of an excuse, but none come to mind, instead, all he can say is, "So, if that's the case, then why did last night happen?". Clio chuckles, confusing him even more, only for her to say, "last night wasn't about you Harry, it was about what I wanted to do, what desires I wanted to fulfill". Harry doesn't know what to say, what to think. On one hand he got the chance to have a threesome with two women who he finds extremely sexy, but then Clio's comment makes it sound like he was a pawn in their game. Should he care? He got what he would have wanted, and so did they, but at the same time, was he manipulated into being a spare part? He lies there, confused, before finally blurting out, "So, what now?". Clio gives out a little laugh, knowing that she is making him squirm.

"Nothing" she tells him, before adding, "We carry on our lives as per normal". Harry seems relieved, thinking that Clio was going to go mad at him, but still, she remains calm and in control, as she continues to smile wryly at him. Harry notices this and his mind wonders why she is being so calm about knowing his infidelities. Clio too knows that the cards are in her favour. She too has played around, and even before finding out about what Harry and Elizabeth have been up to, but she is not about to let that advantage slip. "Why are you being so calm about this?" he finally asks her. Clio continues to smile at him, and then, using the moment to her advantage, she moves the covers down from the bed and climbs between his legs to start pleasuring him with her mouth.

Harry forgets for a moment about the calmness, thinking to himself that maybe Clio has been turned on by thinking about her husband with another woman, and maybe, that's why she told him and Elizabeth to join together so she could watch. Was it that reason?

"When did you find out?" Harry asks. Clio thinks for split seconds, deciding to change the dates, it was of course only yesterday, but thinking about what she has done, she decides to place the date of finding out about a week before she went to the hotel room with Elizabeth. She wants to keep the advantage, the ball in her court.

As Clio works her magic on a moaning Harry, she uses this as the right time to reveal why. As she continues to please him with her mouth, between the action, she starts to tell him. "When I found out about you and her, I was quite mad at you, so I decided to have some fun of my own". Harry thinks about what she has said, but he is too caught up in the moment to get angry or annoyed, how could he? Right now, Clio has him so turned on that she could say almost anything. She will deal with the fall out later, but she knows that she is in the perfect position to carry on telling him.

"First, I went with Elizabeth to a hotel, where I was tied up, then taken by two men. I didn't even get to see who they were, but they used me, and I liked it, no, I loved it!" she tells him, continuing her actions.

Harry is not able to think straight, especially due to the fact that his wife is between his legs and pleasing him. "I can see that hearing that turns you on my love!" as she continues. Harry doesn't know what to think, except to like back and take what Clio is offering, whilst listening to what she has done. "Fair's fair!" is all he can say, thinking that he will accept it. "That's not all" she adds, continuing her work. "I then went with Elizabeth to a car park and watched her have sex with several men". Harry is dazed and confused by now, his mind taking in what she has said, but still unable to react as he doesn't want her to stop what she is doing. "Does that turn you on?" she asks him. He nods his head in agreement, whether he likes it or not. He manages to muster enough control to ask her, "And what about you? Did you just watch?". Clio chuckles as she continues to keep Harry under her control with her mouth, then mumbles enough for him to hear her say, "Not at first. One of them came over and had wis wicked way with me, from behind, over the car bonnet. And then another, then another, and another. I let them all take me, one at a time, until they had all had their turn".

Harry's feelings are now spiraling in his head. On one hand, he should be angry, devastated in fact, to hear that his wife has let one man after another take her, on the other hand, he has his wife between his legs, keeping him under control, making him so turned on by what he is hearing. "Would you like to do that with me Harry?" she asks him. "Would you like to drive me to a secluded spot and watch man after man take me like that?". Harry mumbles that he would, but then again, right now he is not thinking straight. After her last comment, Harry comes to a happy ending, with Clio smirking broadly to herself. Not only has she managed to control her feelings for now on the matter, but she has also revealed to Harry that she knows about him and Elizabeth, they have both slept with Elizabeth together, and she has revealed that she has slept with a handful of men on two separate occasions. After they have concluded their morning activity, Harry begrudgingly tells her that whilst he isn't happy about her having slept with those men, he accepts the blame.

Later that day when the coast is clear, Harry knocks on Elizabeths door, who duly answers. "Hello stud, how can I help you? Have you come back for another round?" she teases him. Harry though is clearly not in the mood for games. "Why the hell didn't you mention that you took my wife out to that hotel and car park?". Elizabeth is shocked that he knows, but also not overly surprised that it has come to light. She quickly counters, "And us fooling around has all been innocent?". Harry snaps back, "That's not the point Elizabeth. Yes, we have been messing about, but not with a whole bunch of other men involved, she could have been in danger, not to mention if they used protection or not, how could you do this?". Elizabeth keeps calm as she replies to his torrent of abuse with, "Harry, it doesn't matter what way you look at it, no one has been an angel here. You win some you lose some. In this case, neither you or Clio comes out as a winner, or the innocent party, you just need to accept it I'm afraid". Harry thinks about what she has said, then mumbles something under his breath that Elizabeth cannot understand before Harry begrudgingly turns away to walk back home. Elizabeth watches him walk away, sensing that this won't be the last time the topic comes up. She knows this and plans for it.

Its Halloween night, and some of the friends have made plans to take their children out trick or treating.
Dom and Nicole, along with Maddie and Phil, have arranged to take their children around to the local houses to bag themselves some treats. As they take their children from house to house, they discuss what they are doing later that evening. Both couples announce that they don't have any post-event plans, and decide that, at short notice, one of them will try to get a babysitter so that they can go to the other persons house, depending on who is successful in finding one at short notice.
Meanwhile, Harry and Clio have taken theirs locally to do the same, along with John and Lynda.
As they go from home to home, Harry talks to Clio about the recent events as he cannot shake the thoughts out from his head. He waits for a quiet time to speak to her.

"Clio, can we talk?" Harry asks her as the children ring the doorbell of the umpteenth house. "Of course, what is it?" she asks him. "It's about you know what, those nights you were with Elizabeth, you know where too" he continues. Clio doesn't look at him as she replies, "What about them?". Harry scoffs, "Well, I know I've done wrong, but don't you think you took it a bit far by deciding to take on a group of complete strangers?!". Clio snorts and replies, "And what, would you prefer that it was with someone you knew? At least I didn't know them Harry, unlike you!". Harry pauses for a moment, knowing that she is at least right in that respect, and searches his thoughts for an appropriate response. It is quite apparent that their relationship hasn't been the same since they have both found out about each other. Harry's attitude doesn't help either, refusing to let it go, but soon realises that everything isn't all as it seems. Finally, Harry breaks the silence, losing his temper as he just about manages to control the volume of his voice. "Well, I can accept that a like for like is fair game considering, I just didn't expect you to act like a whore to a bunch of men you don't know, you might as well have been paid if that was the case, make something out if it" he tells her, his voice angry and full of sarcasm. Clio darts her eyes at him, her face filled with anger, controlled at least in public. She turns to him and replies quietly, "How dare you talk to me like that! How the hell do you think you are?!". Harry looks straight ahead and whispers, "A cheap whore obviously". Clio, still in control of her public emotions, but boiling inside, decides to come clean, to spite him and hurt him for his comments. "Do you know what Harry? I didn't sleep with them because I thought I was spiting you, I slept with them despite NOT knowing about you and Elizabeth. Yes, that's right, I've been whoring it up for months and all this time you were doing the same" she scoffs at him with plenty of sarcasm of her own on the side. "And do you know what? I loved every single second, from one man to the next, feeling them empty everything they had, no protection, I felt everything".

Harry is instantly enraged and turns to face her, grabbing her shoulder to spin her around to face him, and the split second she is, he slaps her hard across the face, sending her head flying sideways. After a moment, Clio gathers herself and moves her head back up to look at Harry in shock. He has never laid a finger on her like that before, but something inside him has snapped. "HOW DARE YOU!" she screams at him. Harry looks at her cheek, which is by now starting to swell, red in colour and scratches on it too from the impact of his strike. Before anyone had a chance to respond, Harry tells her, "I don't regret doing that, I should have done that a long time ago". Clio is now a mixture of emotions; scared, angry, and remorse being some of them. "If it wasn't for Elizabeth, none of this would have happened" he tells her. "If it wasn't her Harry then it would have been someone else, if there hasn't already been so?" she states. Harry turns to walk away to leave her to deal with the children. "Where are you going?!" she demands from him. "To give our neighbour double of what I just gave you, I'm going to bloody kill the bitch". Clio is shocked by his outburst. She knows that he is an arrogant man, but she has not seen this side of him before. Worried about Elizabeth, Clio quickly calls her to warn her that Harry is on the warpath and looking for a fight. She tells Elizabeth what Harry had just said, fearing that he might do something stupid. "Don't worry, I won't answer the door" Elizabeth tells her over the phone. "But what if he tries to do something stupid? Shouldn't we call the police?" Clio asks her. Elizabeth pauses for a moment over the phone and replies, "No police".

The hours pass by, then midnight strikes. Clio is at home with the children. She phones Elizabeth to see what happened, but Elizabeth tells her that she never saw Harry, he never came over. Clio, although angry, starts to worry about what he has done or where he has gone to. She is about to phone her friends but then she is greeted by a knock on the door. "Hi Clio, can we come in?". Inspector Matthews asks her, accompanied by Carter.

November part 2:
There Are No Saints

"Wow, that was a heavy night!" Dom tells Nicole, who is moaning from a hangover. "Christ where are we?" she asks him. "We stayed over at Phil and Maddie's house; don't you remember?" he asks her. Clearly not. "Oh God, how drunk were we last night?" she asks him. "I'd say it was more than just the drink" as he points to an unfinished line of marching powder sitting on their bedside table. Nicole groans and reaches for a glass beside them, only to realise that its champagne. "Oh God, I don't need this at this time of morning, not in this state!" she declares, as Dom laughs. "Do you remember anything about last night?" Dom asks her, with a knowing smirk on his face. "Oh, what happened?!" she asks him, staring to wonder why he is grinning. "Oh, not much, we came back here, had some drinks and some coke and weed, then Phil and I watched you and Maddie put on a bit of a show!" he tells her. "Oh God, did we?!" she asks him, now slightly recalling their antics. "Yes! But you girls made Phil and I bloody kiss first to get you to do it!". Nicole laughs as she now recalls some of the antics. "I bet you loved it secretly!" she tells him, chuckling to herself. "No, not really! Besides, too much stubble too!" he laughs back. "Is that all that happened?" she asks him, trying to recall if they did anything further. "No, not to my knowledge, after that we danced and you ladies passed out, ending the show and potentially seeing more!" he tells her.

As they get up to dress, their phones ping with a message in their group chat. It's from Clio. "Harry died overnight x" it reads.
"Oh my God!" they both say to each other in shock. A minute later, Phil and Maddie burst into their room and ask if they have seen the message, to which they reply that they have. "I can't believe it, I just can't, we only saw him last night!" Maddie sobs, as Nicole comforts her, with Phil and Dom looking devastated by the news. All the friends begin to text each other in their sub-groups, asking how.

Josh is the only one who seems to know any details as he replies that he thinks it was a hit and run as Harry was walking home. All he knows is that it was after midnight and that he was walking across the square when he was hit on Market Place. He goes on to say that the police are currently looking through the CCTV footage to see if they can capture the car details. Steve asks how he knows this information, as Steve is usually enjoys being the first to know something. Josh replies that he can't say who told him as its confidential but its from a reliable source, most likely of course from his friend Inspector Matthews, not that he would commit to passing information on publicly without a full investigation.

Later that morning, all the friends rally round and bring flowers and cards to drop off to Clio's house. She is nowhere to be seen but a family member thanks them for bringing the gifts over, telling them that she is too upset to talk to anyone at this time, understandably.

Meanwhile, later that day, Matthews and Carter are back at the police station after a long night dealing with the death of Harry and having had some much-needed sleep. "This is now far too much of a coincidence" Matthews tells Carter. "What do you mean sir?" she asks him. Mathews looks at her and says, "Look at this and I'll go through it with you". He opens the reports from earlier, then opens a folder on his laptop on the deaths of those from the last eleven months in Hitchin, especially the names of those who are all part of the same circle of friends. He gets a pen and large piece of paper and begins to draw the people that have died so far from the group of friends, explaining to Carter that all the deaths he is showing her, come from that friendship group. As he links the names and where they died, dates and timings, and who they are closely linked with, he starts to visualize a pattern, but he still feels as if a piece of the jigsaw is missing. Carter takes a closer look too as they discuss theories. "I think it could be time to organise a set of interviews with all of them" she declares.

"I can see the information before me, and something is right there, I just can't put my finger on the missing link to tie it all in. It's all there, I know it is" she concludes.

Matthews nods in agreement, telling her that he feels the same, but something is still missing. "OK, let's arrange to bring them all in, one at a time.

Carter and Matthews begin planning, sorting out who they will speak to first, then, over the next couple of days, they visit each friend's home.

First, they go to visit Josh, as Matthews and Josh are old friends and Matthews knows he can trust Josh to be the most honest with him.

Mid conversation, Matthews says, "Mate, between us, you are not a suspect! In fact, at this point, no one is, but there's a link here, something is staring us in the face, but we are missing that spark that will ink everything together". Josh nods in agreement and replies, "To be honest mate, I think it has shaken everyone up a bit, it's more than a coincidence now. Could we be the target of a gang? Maybe some professionals of some sort?". Matthews looks at Carter as they both shakes their heads and he replies, "No, none of this has the hallmarks of a gang, more like, opportunity. Until we find the missing link, and we do have some suspicions, we cannot act on it until then". Carter adds, "If you can think of anything at all, please let us know, we are nearly there on these mysteries". Josh nods at them to say that he will. Matthews knows that Josh is no snitch, and that Josh and the others all have their skeletons too, but he also knows that Josh is not exactly going to cover up a friend if they turn out to be involved in some way for the deaths of some of his friends too.

Next, they pay a visit to Geoff and Claire. They receive similar information from them, based on their whereabouts and what their locations were on the days of each murder. Like Josh and Judith, Geoff and Claire are honest as possible as they can be, letting Matthews and Carter know the information and evidence needed to show that they are not involved.

The same pattern also occurs to Andrew and Katie too. As Matthews and Carter are about to leave, Andrew does pull Matthews to one side and mentions that he assumes Matthews knows about what him and Katie get up to in their private lives, their swinging ways. "Please tell me this isn't an invite!" Matthews quips. Andrew chuckles as he says it's not, but he does share that he thinks that some of the others might have a web of activity with each other. "What do you mean?" Matthews asks him. "Well, I am not certain, but I think I may have seen our neighbours at a club that we go to". Matthews interest piques as he replies, "What neighbours would that be?". Katie joins in with, "We don't want to stitch them up of course because what people get up to in their private lives is their business, but we can at least tell you the club and dates that we have been". Matthews looks at Carter, who nods back at him, as Matthews also nods and begins to take some notes down.

Throughout the day and the next day, Matthews and Carter visit the remaining couples to make enquiries with them to ask about their whereabouts over the recent months, suggesting that they might want to show some form of evidence or at least confirm the dates of their locations. This is something they have already done with some of them, but a fresh approach will not hurt their investigation, especially as they can cross reference their notes from the previous encounters.
The people visited include:
Steve and Kirsty, Dominic and Nicole, Phil and Maddie, John and Lynda, Elizabeth and James, Clio, and Indya.

"I feel like most of them have something to hide" Matthews tells Carter. "Agreed sir, question is, is it hiding something seedy about themselves or is it something more?". Matthews agrees with a nod before adding, "Come on, let's get back to the station, I think we've got some more digging to do".

At the police station, Matthews and Carter begin to revisit some of the CCTV footage saved on file, and they collect other data based on information shared with them.
"Sir, come and look at this" she tells him. As he leans over to view some CCTV footage he asks her, "Where is this?". She replies with a wry smile, "This is at the club that Katie and Andrew like to visit", referring to the swinger's club. "You're not about to show me some sordid action, are you?" Matthews asks her, smiling and raising an eyebrow. Carter half laughs as she replies she in not, but adds, "Look at the cars parked outside, this one in particular". Matthews looks at it and the number plate and says, "OK, do we know this car?". Carter then opens another file to show CCTV footage from the night that Sebastian was killed in the apparent mugging". Matthews looks at both videos and confirms it is the same car but then adds, "But Sebastian was stabbed in the alleyway, wasn't he?". Carter nods but adds, "But when you rewind the footage back to earlier in the day, look where the suspect is". Matthews looks closer at the footage, only to see that the suspect in question, is leaning through the open window of the same car as seen at the swinger's club. "Christ! The same car!" he declares. "Great work Carter, really good work. I think we should first try to find out the owner of that car, then maybe dig back at the other murders and see if that car is linked. "On it sir" Carter replies. Matthews adds, "Lets revisit the details in order of murder, see if that pulls up any clues".

Later, Carter reports back to Matthews with news on the murders. "Sir, for Enrique's murder, there is no sign of the car involved, but I did contact the doorbell company that he used, and that has shown him being murdered by someone. We cannot see the face, but we were able to make out a couple of features". Matthews looks at the pictures and video and asks her to continue, intrigued and pleased with Carter's attention to details. "Look here" she tells him. "The murderer has a very specific footwear underneath all the clothing he or she has clearly worn to try and cover themselves up".

Matthews looks and adds, "It's as if they clearly did not want any part of them to be seen". Carter replies, "Well, that would be quite obvious considering they were murdering someone!". Matthews chuckles gently before adding, "Yeah, true, but this person has taken extra steps, which leads me to believe that maybe Enrique knew the murderer, and if it didn't work out, then Enrique would not be able to identify who it was". Carter looks back at the screen, intrigued and looking closely to find any more clues.

Matthews picks up a pen and begins to write the names of all four victims on the see-through Perspex board.

"OK, so let's run by them again" Matthews says to Carter. "Sebastian was murdered on 14th of February".

Carter says, "Valentines Day" of course".

Matthews continues, "Enrique, on 31st of March".

Carter again chips in with, "Clocks went forward".

Matthews nods as he then writes, "Rebecca on 20th June".

Carter again chips in with, "Longest day of the year".

By now Matthews is slightly irritated by her chipping in, but not to the point of annoyance, but just to flash her a knowing look, almost a smirk, to which she smiles back and raises her eyebrows, showing that she doesn't care! Matthews finishes with, "Harry on Halloween" then turns to look at Carter, thinking he has beaten her to it, to which she smiles and appreciates the humour. Carter chips in once more but this time to be more serious, "Actually sir, the evidence and timings show it was just after midnight, so he would be the 1st of November".

Matthews and Carter stare at the names as another colleague enters the room. "Matthews, Carter" he greets them. "Hi Sir" they greet back. "So, how's the cases coming along?" he asks them. "We have the jigsaw pieces but not the picture to make it" Matthews replies. "Well, if you need…". Just then his phone rings, as Matthews and Carter watch on. "Yes yes, I'm on my way!" he replies down the phone. "Sorry old chaps, must dash, the wife has just pranged the car". Carter replies, "Oh, sorry to hear that sir, can we help?". He shakes his head and tuts, followed by,

"Only God can help her with this one! The insurance will be through the roof now!" he snorts as he exits the room. Carter chuckles as she watches him leave then turns to Matthews. He is not watching or looking at either of them. "What?" she asks him. "Oh my God, I think I've got it!" Matthews tells her. Carter's eyes open wide as she asks him how. "The dates, it's all in the dates!" he replies, almost excitedly, before adding, "But first, we need more evidence, concrete evidence".

Matthews quickly goes to his laptop and contacts the DVLA to see the previous owners of the car used in the murders. He sees that it is registered to someone called George Richards. Carter sees the details and tries to call the number but the tone id dead. Matthews then finds the number of the local police station to where the last address of this George Richards is from.
"Hi, this is Inspector Matthews of Hertfordshire Police, I am after some information if you can help?" he asks down the phone. Carter waits patiently as she listens to the muffled conversation. As Matthews speaks, he pauses, looks at Carter, says his thanks and goodbyes then hangs up.
"He's dead" Matthews tells Carter. "Well, there's a surprise!" Carter replies. Just then, an email pops up in Matthews's account, to which he opens and shows Carter the picture of George Richards. "This is him, he died last year". Carter looks at him and says, "And?" expecting more from his response. "And..." Matthews says, "he died on the 25th of July... allegedly mugged". Carter looks at him and studies his excited eyes, his mouth almost smiling at having worked out the clues. She goes to her laptop and types in all the detail and now sees the pattern. "Oh my God, you don't think..." but Matthews cuts in with, "I do yes!". Carter can hardly believe it as Matthews grabs his coat, prints off some pictures of George Richards, the car, a picture of another person, quicky grabs them and opens the door to leave. "Come on Carter!" as she too grabs her coat, almost as excited as him to get going.

Matthews and Carter take a short drive over the county border and pull up to an unspecified address.

"Hello, I wondered of you could help me" Matthews asks the person who greeted them at the door he knocked on. "Yes? Who are you?" the lady asks. Carter jumps in with, "Sorry Miss, we are from the police, I am Inspector Matthews, and this is Carter, we are trying to trace the owner of this car". The lady takes the picture and gives it a quick glance before handing it back to them. "This was George's car, why do you ask?" she asks. Carter then plays it with a softer tone and asks, "Miss, this car has been seen in CCTV footage over the last few months, and we believe it is connected to a series of deaths in Hitchin". The lady looks at them both and replies, "Well it clearly isn't my George, he's dead you know, died last year, summertime". Matthews smiles gently at her and replies, "We are sorry for the loss of your husband". The lady looks at him and replies sharply, "You don't have to try to charm the knickers off me you know, I think its quite clear that I am too old to be his wife, or sister for that matter". Matthews bows his head as a way of apology, as the lady turns her head to Carter and replies with a wink and a small smile, "Since he's quite handsome I'll let him off!". Carter smiles broadly as Matthews smiles too, nodding his head in appreciation of her quick wit.

The lady continues, "My George used to work in some seedy little club but was laid off, so he sold the car to make some money". Carter looks at Matthews then at the lady to ask, "Do you know who to?". The lady shakes her head as she replies, "He sold it for cash, that's what the man buying it insisted on". Matthews and Carter again look at each other, then Matthews pulls out a picture and asks, did the person look like this?". The lady takes the picture and says, "Yes, yes, it is, how do you know?". Carter replies with, "This person is now our primary suspect". The lady replies with, "Ooh! Well, good luck with that one!". Matthews and Carter smile at the lady as they make their back to their own car. "Officers!" she calls out to them, George had a garage too, quite near Hitchin too". Matthews and Carter grin as they look at each other.

Matthews and Carter reach the station back in Hitchin as they set to work on finding out where the garage that had George's car is located. They contact the local council to find out about the garage and give George's name as the last registered owner. "Uh huh, OK, thanks" as Matthews slams the phone down, scribbling an address at the same time. "Come on, let's go check this place out" he tells Carter.

As they pull up to a block of garages, Carter gets out and checks the area, then pulls out a skeleton key that matches the size of the padlock on the garage.

They partially open the garage door, and behold, the car in the CCTV footage is there in front of them. "Bingo!" Carter declares, as Matthews grins and pushes the door fully open. They both pull out rubber gloves to make sure they don't cross contaminate, then start to inspect the vehicle. "Carter, can you get hold of forensics and ask them to get down here at the double?". Carter nods as she gets her phone out to make the call. Matthews looks on, almost excited at the prospect of nearing the end of the biggest mystery of his career to date.

About twenty minutes later, one of the forensics team arrive. They put on their suit, mask, and gloves, then proceed to swab the car in places that Matthews asks them too, putting the swabs into sealed bags and labelled. Matthews then opens the car boot. "Well, well, well!" he declares to Carter, looking at her as she looks into the boot too. "Looks like the clothing of the person identified on the doorbell footage from Enrique's house!" she replies. The forensics personnel then swab the clothing and finds blood stains on it, and some hairs too, that they bag up along with the other evidence.

Matthews then pulls out a metallic looking item and passes it to Carter, who also notices the blood stains on its base. Carter looks and Matthews and smiles as she tells him, "You know where you'll find one of these don't you?" telling him, rather than asking him. Matthews smiles back as he nods in agreement, as Carter passes the item to forensics for testing.

After an hour, Matthews, Carter, and Forensics, close the garage and lock it back up. As they do so, another colleague of Matthews and Carter arrive and begin to install a hidden camera, pointing at the garage door. Carter checks the feed and asks the technician to report back to her the moment the sensors alert her colleague.

"What now, shall we go and pay this person a visit?" Carter asks. Matthews pauses for a moment and replies, "No, unfortunately not, not without the results from forensics to come back, and that could take weeks as we are dealing with multiple cases, and we want to be 100% sure we've got the right person". She looks at him and nods to agree. She then asks, "How about some surveillance then?". Matthews nods in agreement and asks her to arrange some, especially whilst they are in the process of waiting for all evidence to come back to them. "Sir, I've just though of something though. We might find the samples to match the DNA of the victims, but how can we prove that the murderers DNA will match the suspect? We can't just march in and take it from them?". Matthews stops walking and turns to look at her. "We don't have to! I've already done it!". Carter looks quite surprised and asks him how.

"Remember when we paid each person a visit to their homes to ask them all questions?". Carter nods that she does. "And do you remember me asking for a cup of tea and a glass of water each time?". Carter again nods in agreement. "And do you remember me always asking to swap seats in their front rooms with them each time they sat down as I said I loved their sofa's and was on the look out for a new one and wanted to see what they were like?" By now Carter is becoming bored at his lack of getting to the point. "OK, so each time they left the room, I made sure that I found as many hairs as possible from their chairs, and I found a whole bunch, and, inside the clothing that was in the car boot, there were hairs on the inside too". Carter by now is twigging. "So, all we need to do is match the hairs from each house to the hairs found inside the clothing" she asks. "Exactly!" he replies with a smile.

December:
Jingle All You Slay

December, the month of Christmas, party season, spending too much money, getting fat, drunk, stoned, high, or, in some cases, arrested for multiple murders!

The circle of friends of Hitchin's self-made high society have arranged a special night out at Santorini's for a Christmas party and to celebrate Judith's birthday too. The friends all gather and sit in their little groups as the wine flows, the food is endless, as is the popping of champagne corks too. They have all chipped in to hire a top DJ for the night too, to make it extra special, to see out the year in style, but to also toast those friends that are missing.
Kirsty stands up and breaks up the chatter to announce, "A toast, to us all, for Christmas, to get over this torrid year of events and to put the past behind us and hope that next year will be a better one… and hopefully no one dies!".
Some of the friends laugh, some chuckle, but one or two find it a little distasteful. This is down to the fact that even though it is a big circle of friends, not everyone is the best of friends in some cases, or maybe it's just that some comments are best not said.
As they sit down, Josh breaks the silence with, "So, here's to my wife, happy birthday darlin!", doing his best to bring the focus back to something a little more positive. The friends all smile again as they clink glasses and sip away. After the main meals have been eaten, the men gather in their little huddle, as the women do too.
The men gathered include Josh, Geoff, John, Andrew, Phil, Steve, James, Tom, Tyler, and Dominic.
"So, what have you got Judith for her birthday then Josh?" asks Andrew. Josh replies that he has bought her some nice jewelry, clothes, and a couple of experiences out for them to enjoy together, such as a weekend trip to Rome and another ski trip too.
Geoff and Andrew nod along and smile in approvement. Steve pipes up with, "I've got Kirsty a nice holiday too, I'm going to take her to New York for a few days".

The others smile and nod in agreement that it is a lovely gift.

"What about the rest of you? Any nice plans coming up?" Josh asks politely.

"Well, we are all going skiing again, aren't we?!" Geoff reminds him, especially as it is Josh's birthday next month. "Christ! I can't believe that a year has almost gone by again!". Josh quickly looks over at the reverend James, who chuckles at his comment, with Josh quickly saying, "Sorry James! Didn't mean to blaspheme!". James laughs as he replies, "Don't worry, I have heard much worse" as the friends chuckle together.

Over in the women's group, the ladies chat away and catch up on gossip over recent times. The group includes: Judith, Claire, Katie, Kirsty, Maddie, Nicole, Elizabeth, Clio, Lynda, and Indya.

The ladies chat to Clio, making her the centre of attention for the first part, asking her how she is bearing up and that they will all be there to support her.

Kirsty, tactful as ever, says, "It was a lovely service Clio, Harry would have been proud of that sendoff". The others chip in with their own comments of support to Clio, who seems to be bearing up OK. Elizabeth sits beside her, stroking her hand tenderly under the table, to which Clio doesn't react to, but not pulling her hand away either.

"Anyway" Clio says, "We have carol concert coming up, something to look forward to". The other ladies nod and say that they will all be there. "Elizabeth, I hear that you'll be in the choir!" Claire says with a smile. Elizabeth nods back with a smile and replies, "I am only doing it to support James. There are a million other things I'd much rather be doing", to which Maddie and Nicole finger poke each other's legs under the table as they wryly smile. As the other ladies' chat to each other, Nicole turns to speak to Maddie quietly and asks, "How are you feeling?", to which Maddie replies, "To be honest I'm feeling a bit better this month. The Last two months I've felt a little sick in the morning". Nicole replies, "Well it's that time of year for bug spreading, isn't it?".

Maddie smiles back then tells her softly, "To be honest, I'm a little worried. I've been the most regular person with my monthly cycle, but it's been about three months since my last one". Nicole looks at her and tells her, "Sweetie, we are all at that age now where it could be early menopause. My mother had hers around my age, so it can happen at funny times in our lives". Maddie smiles back at her and replies, "You're probably right" but as Nicole turns to speak to the others, Maddie's face paints a different picture. The biggest worry for her is that she has worked out the timings since her last cycle, and she has concluded that she wasn't having that much romance between the sheets with Phil at that time, and the only other person she has been messing around with was Nicole.

"Sir, we have the reports back from the lab regarding those hair samples" Carter tells Matthews. "Excellent, let's see them!" he replies, pleased that it may reveal some facts to them. He opens the report and reads through it, looking at the DNA tests and who they match to.
"Oh my God!" Carter exclaims, looking at the results. "So, it seems that there is a link to them all after all" Matthews replies, almost happy that his theory has been proved right. "But is it still enough to make an arrest?" Carter asks him. "Almost, but I think I need one or two more pieces of evidence, and I know exactly where to look for them" Matthews says, a glint in his eye to suggest that he has a plan of action. Matthews turns to another colleague and asks her, "Zoe, I need you to contact these two companies and get CCTV footage from these exact dates and rough timings. All other details that you need I've just sent in an email to you". His colleague Zoe looks at him and nods in understanding, replying that she will do so.
"Come on, grab your coat, let's get what we need" he tells Carter, as they hurriedly grab their coats and depart the police station.

A couple of days pass as the various couples continue making their December plans, with a notable carol concert coming up that they are all planning to attend.

The night before the carol concert, Josh, and Judith head over to see Geoff and Claire, along with Katie and Andrew, to have a few drinks and laze around together, catching up and to enjoy some time in the hot tub too. "So, what do you have coming up then?" asks Geoff to the friends, as they all sit in the hot jets of bubbles, holding their various drinks and smoke away on a joint whilst music plays in the background. Josh replies, "Well, I have a wonderful time coming up having to go to the dentist to get more work done on these bloody teeth of mine! It's costing a small fortune! But to be fair, they are good at what they do, and it must be done". Andrew chuckles as he remarks that he too needs to get his checkup booked. "Where do you go then?" Claire asks him. "Tilehouse Dental clinic. No waiting, nice and calm, and the staff put you at ease" Josh replies, then adding, "But I reckon the amount of time I have spent going there, I think its paid for their staff Christmas party!". The friends chuckle as they quickly tun their conversation around to the other friends not present. "I've heard a few rumours recently about some of the others. It feels like there's a few strained relationships" says Katie. Judith adds, "Yes, I've heard and seen that not all is well in some camps, but with everything that's happened over these last twelve months it's not surprising". Andrew adds, "Has there been any updates on the dearly departed?" referring to those that are now deceased from their circle. "Not yet, but I am sure something will come out sooner or later" Josh replies. Claire changes the subject back to the rumours flying around. "So, come on then, what gossip is doing the rounds?" she asks the others, sitting up to prick her ears up to listen in. Katie says, "Well from the sounds of it, and allegedly, Elizabeth has been quite active on the husband front". The others all sit up to listen, eager to hear the gossip. "Ooh! tell more!" Claire asks. Katie adds, "Well I 've overheard the other wives saying things but that's all I know to be honest, besides, if anything is going on then I'm not getting involved!". "Unless she wants to join us!" Andrew chips in with, making the others laugh at his comment.

The day of the carol concert arrives. Josh and Judith are busy getting ready, texting the group to see what everyone else is wearing, based on the weather and if they plan to go elsewhere afterwards for a drink. Replies beep on their phones from various others to show pictures of what they are wearing, the usual quips and jokes, and of course that some are keen to go out afterwards. Whilst Maddie is getting ready, Phil decides to send Elizabeth a private message. "Hey, carol concerts are quite boring don't you think? Fancy making it a bit more exciting?" he writes in his message to her.

At her home, Elizabeth sees the message come through and she smiles to herself as she reads it. Phil is now downstairs in his home, sipping a drink as Maddie continues to potter around upstairs as his phone beeps with a message. He opens it up to see that Elizabeth has replied and has also sent an image, with the message reading, "Do you mean something like this?" which is written underneath an image of her hitched dress, revealing that she is wearing stockings and suspenders. Phil shifts uncomfortably in his set as he smirks and writes a reply that it is exactly what he was thinking of.

One by one the friends arrive in town and first meet at the Hermitage Bar and restaurant for some pre-carol drinks with each other. Everyone greets each other as they sit down and order their drinks and catch up. The hot tub crew sit and listen and give each other knowing smiles as they listen to the conversations and tales from the other friends, but also catching up on what they have been up to over the last few days.

As they talk, Phil sneaks a few glances over at Elizabeth, giving her a wry smile as she remains in control of her responses, but making sure that she has acknowledged his communications.

Meanwhile, things are hotting up at the police station where Matthews and Carter are working hard along with some other colleagues to finalise the arrest warrants.

"Has the CPS come back to us to approve the footage we have and wanted?" Matthews asks Carter. She smiles back and replies, "They have indeed, it's now game on". Matthews smiles back and thanks her. Matthews calls all those now involved with the operation to the conference room to outline what needs to be done. "I am not expecting a big fight, but we still need to be prepared. We just need to have officers stationed at these exit points and to make sure that we have control of the crowd as there will be many people present and confused". PC Sale asks him, "Just to double check, is this the right setting to do this? It's very public". Matthews replies, "I don't think we have much choice, plus it's the only place we know that they will definitely be present". Sale agrees with a nod and takes note. "OK. Any questions?" Matthews asks the small group gathered. No one replies and nods that they are ready. "OK, then let's do this".

Josh, Judith, Claire, Geoff, Katie, Andrew, Steve, Kirsty, Phil, Maddie, Dominic, Nicole, Tom, Tyler, John, Lynda, Clio, Elizabeth, and Indya, all make their way from the Hermitage to the church for the carol concert.
Most of the friends sit near each other along the same pews, with Elizabeth sitting elsewhere in support of her husband James who is conducting the service, with Clio and Indya sitting further forward from the friends, in support of each other, being the widows amongst the group.
The reverend James opens proceedings by welcoming everyone to the carol concert, addressing the congregation as the singers from the choir all make their way to their positions to begin the concert.
As the concert begins and the friends sit and listen, Phil pretends to hold his stomach, faking a bit of stomachache and telling Maddie that he needs to go to the toilet as he feels unwell. She tuts at him as he discreetly makes his way from the pew and to the back of the church. A few moments later, Elizabeth discreetly looks at the message sent to her phone. She reads it then carefully gets up and retreats to where the toilets are located.

"There you are, I've been waiting for this!" Phil tells her. Elizabeth puts a finger to his mouth to stop him from talking further, takes his hand and says, "Follow me, I know where the quiet areas are in this place". Phil does as he is told and follows her lead, a big Cheshire cat smile on his face, using his other hand to grope Elizabeths bottom. Upon reaching a room away from the concert, Elizabeth shuts the door as her and Phil begin to kiss and grope each other. After a few moments of doing so, she tells him, "We don't have much time otherwise people will become suspicious". Phil nods to agree as Elizabeth begins to undo his belt and trousers, quickly puling them down. Phil leans back against a desk as Elizabeth quickly drops to her knees to give Phil a warmup to get him at peak performance. After a minute of doing so, she stands up and hitches her dress up and lets Phil remove her knickers, pulling them down in double time. She wastes no time as she parts her legs and holds on to the desk and commands him to take her now. Phil wastes no time as he moves into position and begins the deed.

Meanwhile, Maddie is now wondering where Phil is, thinking to herself that he is taking a while, although it has only been five minutes since he left, but something is in her head, prompting her to get up and move her way from the pew to the back of the church and to the toilets to check up on him. When she arrives at the toilets, she knocks on the doors to see if he is in there, but after several attempts and no answer, she gets her phone out to call him.
In the other area of the church where Phil and Elizabeth are, his phone begins to ring. He and Elizabeth halt proceedings as he answers it, telling her that he has gone outside to walk around to get some fresh air. "OK, well don't be too long. If you are unwell, I can take you home?" Maddie asks him, "No, no, that's OK, I'll be OK, I just need some air. I went to the toilet but then needed some air".

Maddie hangs up as she is about to make her way back into the main hall, but then notices some movement taking place outside. She moves to the window and sees that it's the police, and quite a few of them too. Before she can think or react, two police officers come through the doorway next to her and stop for a moment to look at her, as one of them looks at a photo in one of their hands, before shaking their head to move off to the next location in the church. Maddie instantly gets her phone out and texts all the friends in their main WhatsApp group to say that the police are swamping the building. Inside the church some of the friends discreetly pull their phones out to see the message then start to look at each other with surprise, wondering where she is and what the police are doing. Maddie decides to follow the two police officers that she just saw, from a slight distance, seeing what they are up to, curious of course, as to why the police are sniffing around a church. On carol concert night.

The only people who haven't looked at the group message of course, is Phil and Elizabeth, who are in the throes of passion in another room.

Maddie sees the police enter another room she follows and watches what they are doing, then, as they turn around to search the room and see her watching, they tell her to back off, so she shies away from view and presses her back against a door, deciding to open it, walking into it backwards.

As she does so, she is greeted by the sounds of grunting and groaning. Quickly she spins around to be greeted by the sight of Phil going ten to the dozen behind a willing Elizabeth.

"PHIL!" she screams out. Phil spins his around instantly to see Maddie staring at him, open mouthed, as Elizabeth turns her head too, to be greeted by the shock on Maddie's face. "Sweetheart I can explain!" he blurts out. Maddie's face turns to one of thunder as she bellows out, "Explain? EXPLAIN? Get lost!" she scowls at him.

Just then, the two police officers that Maddie was watching, enter the room, and quickly check their photo. "'Ello, 'ello, 'ello!" one of them says, with a smirk on their face, witnessing the scene before them, as they walk over to take hold of Elizabeth, who is still in front and connected to a startled Phil.

The first officer tells Phil, "Sir, please step back and disconnect yourself from the women now, please". Phil instantly steps back and does as he is told, hurriedly pulling his trousers up, as the second officer restrains Maddie, who is trying to hit him for what he has done. The second officer begins to put handcuffs on Elizabeth as he says to her, "Elizabeth Valise Tanner, I am arresting you on suspicion of Murder, conspiracy to murder, conspiracy of perverting the course of justice and indecent exposure in a public place. You do not have to say anything, but it may harm your defence if you do not mention when questioned something which you rely on in court. Anything you do say may be given in evidence; do you understand?". Elizabeth nods her head as she complies with the police.

Back in the main body of the church, the choir are blissfully singing away as the crowd watch on, when police officers appear at all the doorways and exit points. At first no one notices until they start to walk forward slowly, then the choir one by one stop signing as the watching crowd start to murmur and talk amongst themselves.

Matthews and Carter walk to the front and straight to the reverend James. "What on earth is going on?" he asks them. "We are in the middle of a concert; you cannot come in here and interrupt in the house of God" he tells them. Matthews and Carter look at him then at each other. Matthews nods at Carter who steps forward.

Carter pulls out a pair of handcuffs and states:

"Cameron Ulysses Nicholas Tanner, I am arresting you on five counts of murder, For the murders of Sebastian Cobmade, Enrique Santow, Rebecca Cobmade, Harry Bonihor and George Richards conspiracy to murder, conspiracy to pervert the course of justice".
She continues,
"I am also arresting you on suspicion of conspiracy to murder, conspiracy of perverting the course of justice and indecent exposure in a public place. You do not have to say anything, but it may harm your defence if you do not mention when questioned something which you rely on in court. Anything you do say may be given in evidence; do you understand?".

The gathered crowd gasp in shock as they watch James being led away outside, to which Josh and the others quickly get up and rush outside to carry on watching to events unfold. As they all reach outside, they see Elizabeth in handcuffs too, being ushered towards a police car, and of course an enraged Maddie who is still trying to hit and punch Phil, who is being guarded by a police officer, who threatens to arrest Maddie if she carries on.

"What the hell is going on?!" the friends ask each other. Josh managed to approach Matthews and asks him what is going on. "James, the reverend, he killed them all, with help from his wife". Josh's mouth drops as he watches the scenes unfold around him. "Sorry mate, I need to get these two down to the station, I'll catch up with you later" Matthews tells him. Josh nods his head and thanks Matthews. Judith goes over to Josh and asks what is going on. "James and Elizabeth, they did it, they killed them all". Judith is shocked and asks, "What?! Are you saying they killed all our friends?!". Josh nods his head to say yes. By now the other friends come over as the group begins to talk amongst themselves, in disbelief at what is going on. Clio begins to well up as she looks at Elizabeth in the back of the police car, guarded, along with James in another car also guarded, as the rest of the police begin removing artefacts from the church.

Once the commotion begins to settle down, the friends make their way back to the Hermitage Bar to talk about what they have witnessed.

Josh tells the friends, "So from I can gather, it was James all along who was the mastermind behind the murders, and Elizabeth helped him". Claire chips in with, "I can't believe that we've had a serial murderer amongst us all this time". As the friends continue to talk, Clio remains rather silent as she listens on. Kirsty asks her, "How are you feeling about all this?". Clio mumbles something but doesn't make total sense, perhaps being in a state of shock still. Lynda comes over to give Clio a cuddle and to put a hand on Indya's shoulder in reassurance too, who is not herself, but would she? Having just heard that two people who infiltrated their circle of friends only 12 months ago, are responsible for killing her husband, Clio's husband, Sebastian, and Rebecca too, and some other poor soul who they don't know.

Clio breaks down crying and then admits to Lynda that she had been having an affair with Elizabeth. "Oh…!" Lynda replies, not quite knowing what to say next. All she can do is give her a cuddle. Clio really is in a mess. Maddie too is upset, having witnessed firsthand what her husband had been doing, as the women also console her. Everything has concluded in this one big mess of deceit, but it hasn't ended yet.

Whilst the women rally around Clio and Indya, the men talk amongst themselves. As some of them chatter away about the days events, unsurprisingly, Phil has decided to swerve this gathering, having gone home with his tail tucked between his legs, having been caught out with Elizabeth in the act.

"So how long has it been going on between Phil and Elizabeth?" Geoff and Andrew ask Josh. "I don't know, for all we know that could be the tip of the iceberg, I mean, we know that she is a flirty woman, but quite clearly a lot more dangerous than we knew!" Josh replies to them. It comes as no shock that Steve and Dominic are fairly quiet and listen to the conversations rather than join in, after all, they too have their dirty little secrets involving Elizabeth.

Christmas comes and goes as the various groups spend it in their own way. The circle of friends has become fractured due to the events that have taken place, culminating in the rather high-profile arrests of two of the friends and the deaths of four of them, by the hands of the afore mentioned two people. It is something that none of them saw coming nor thought about, especially as there were never any signs of murderous intent or behaviour to suggest otherwise.

The new year takes place, with people going about their daily lives still, until the date of the court case for James and Elizabeth is announced.
The group of friends make their plans to attend the hearings, to sit in the public gallery.
The first day arrives and the friends make their way either solo or in small groups to the crown court to watch how it all happened. As James and Elizabeth arrive in court and sit in the dock, the friends look over at them, some with blank faces, some with scorn, especially Clio and Indya for obvious reason. The opening speeches are given by both the defence and the prosecution, then evidence is given. The ladies sit alongside each other, with Clio and Indya in the middle of them, sort of like a comfort blanket for them. The men sit one row back, behind their wives. Maddie has turned up, but no sign of Phil. Katie turns to Maddie to ask how she is. Maddie is quite stoic, but her eyes betray her true feelings as she says that she is OK, that her and Phil are sleeping in separate rooms too. Katie looks down and notices that Maddie has a growing bump. Katie looks back at her to ask, "Maddie, I don't want to be rude but…" and before she can finish, Maddie nods to say that she is, in fact, pregnant. Katie holds her hand to comfort her. Maddie then turns to her and says, "The problem is, the timings don't match up with Phil, so I don't know what's going on". Katie does her best to comfort her as the proceedings of the court continue around them.

The next day, the prosecution lay out all the evidence for all to see, making it quite clear what has happened.

The lead prosecutor provides the dates that all the murders too place on.
- February 14th. Most would think of this as Valentines Day, but it is also the same day as the start of lent. The day Sebastian was murdered.
- 31st March. The day the clocks go forward to commence British Summer Time, but also Easter Sunday. The day Enrique was murdered.
- 20th June. The longest day of the year, summer solstice. Celebrated in some Christian circles, but also contains a pagan side to it too. The day Rebecca was murdered.
- 1st November. The day after Halloween. All Saints Day. The day that Harry was murdered.
- And the year before, the 1st of December, the start of advent, George, the unknown person to the friend's group, was murdered.

The prosecution talks about how the sadistic reverend waited for the dates to come and pick them as times to kill the people that he did, as if it was his calling card. It is said that many serial killers like to leave breadcrumbs, as a way of goading the authorities, but with most, they end up being caught because of them.
James is no different in this case.

The prosecution continues its evidence.
They speak to the court to explain how James had bought the car that he used as an accessory to go about un-noticed, from a man called George. James paid cash for the car, but it was registered under his real name of Cameron. This caused an issue to the police at the time as James had changed his name from Cameron to James to hide his murky past.
The trouble was that Georges mother was able to identify James from pictures when shown to her by Matthews and Carter.

Once they could ID the car and that it was James who had bought it, they were able to retrieve CCTV footage from surrounding areas close to each murder and see that for the murder of Sebastian, James was seen in the car in another part of town handing money to the person who committed the murder, someone who to date hasn't been captured, yet.

The next evidence to back it up is CCTV footage taken from the storage banks of the in-house cameras that James and Elizabeth had. These were installed in their home for their own perverse reasons, to fil themselves having extra martial relations with anyone and everyone who displayed an interest. When this is mentioned, several of the men in the friends group begin to shuffle in their seats uncomfortably.

It also picked up the conversations between James and Elizabeth about the murder and subtle hints at what happened and how it happened.

It transpired that Matthews was able to obtain evidence from another bordering police force that James was in fact formally known as Cameron as they had him on file for indecent acts in a public place and were able to share the information to him to use as evidence.

The car too was seen on CCTV footage obtained from the swinger's club and from the car park that Elizbeth took Clio to. It turns out that the mystery driver that night was James. Once this information is read out, it dawns on Clio that one of the men who had sex with her must have been James, making her recoil in horror and begin to sob in the gallery.

It was also shown that James and Elizabeth were in fact members of this swinger's club and that the CCTV footage shows his car there on many occasions, making it damning evidence that he is in fact the owner and driver. More evidence shows that the same shoes and imprints from James's shoes shows that it is a close match to finding footprints at a couple of the murder scenes, notably Harry and Rebecca's.

A candle stick holder was taken from the church and shown to have spots of blood on it, notably from Harry's DNA, showing that he must have bene hit hard over the head with it.
More CCTV footage taken from James and Elizabeths home shows that James was wearing the same clothing used when he killed Harry and Enrique. James's mistake here was not getting rid of them, but this is another indicator of his hidden arrogance.

DNA was taken from underneath Rebecca's fingernails, showing that it now matched James's DNA, and that small strands of hair were found at James's home on his sofa, something that Matthews noticed and took for testing. Hairs were also found on the same clothing used by James for when he killed Harry.

Then, all hell breaks loose with the images and videos that have been captured by the police to use as evidence.

The first pictures and videos show Elizabeth and Enrique together inside Santorini's nightclub getting up to no good. Indya is shocked by this and begins to break down crying.

Footage is then played from Sebastian's old phone files taken from the cloud, showing Elizabeth kicking the man in the night club in the head, putting him the coma.

Next is the footage of James driving and handing over the cash to the man to kill Sebastian.

More footage shows Harry and Elizabeth engaging in sexual acts in her home, with James secretly watching in another room, getting his kicks from doing so.

Video footage taken from James's doorbell camera shows him in the same clothing shown to be worn by the person who killed Enrique, which was James of course.

A video is then shown of Steve entering the house, let in by Elizabeth, and then footage of them performing all kinds of acts is shown in the court. Kirsty at this point begins to cry as she turns around to confront Steve, who bows his head down to avoid eye contact. Kirsty is livid but does enough to hold her emotions at bay, whilst inside the court room.

Text messages take from Elizabeths phone shows the exchange of photos and messages sent by Rebecca and Sebastian, showing that they know what she was up to, which prompted the police to look further into her activities which then highlighted the reverend even more so.

Footage from James and Elizabeths home then reveals that Phil had engaged in sexual acts long before he was caught in December, prompting Maddie to become enraged in the gallery. By now, Kirsty, Maddie and Indya are livid, upset, angry, confused, all the emotions you can imagine.

Then a huge bombshell. Footage is then shown in James and Elizabeths home of Phil and Maddie entering, then the CCTV footage from inside shows Phil and Elizabeth having sex whilst Maddie is passed out, something she semi-remembers from that night, but is then horrified to see James having sex with her whilst she is passed out. The friends gasp in horror as it dawns upon them that Maddie is now quite clearly pregnant, and she has confided that she thinks the timings with when she and Phil had been sleeping together don't add up, which at first made her confused. Not anymore. Maddie now realises that a murderer has made her pregnant.

Then footage from September emerges, showing that Elizabeth has a threesome with Harry and Phil. This shocks the friends again. By now, Maddie and Clio are sobbing and have to leave the courtroom, quickly followed by Claire and Katie, who do their best to console them.

A video is shown of James driving and participating in an outdoor dogging spot, and Clio is clearly made out in the pictures. The gallery, especially the friends, gasp in audible shock as they realise that Clio has been messing around.

Video footage is then shown inside James and Elizabeths home of them talking about how to kill Harry, and that James will again take care of it.

Footage also emerges of Dominic and Elizabeth also meeting up to engage in sexual activities.
At this point, all the wives have now left the gallery and gone outside, some crying, some trying to comfort the others. It has now become a tangled web of lies and cheating, plus spoonful's of deceit, and the common theme in all of them is Elizabeth.

Josh, Geoff, Andrew, John, Tom, and Tyler, look at the other friends who have now been exposed as Elizabeths playthings. Steve and Dominic look rather sheepishly to the floor. Phil of course is not present as he has already been found out.

After the day's proceedings conclude, the men and women of the friends group make their way to various locations. Josh and Judith head out to The Lytton Arms in Knebworth along with Geoff, Claire, Andrew, Katie, John, Lynda, Tom, and Tyler.
Dominic and Steve respectively have headed straight home with their wives Nicole and Kirsty, to face the music, and for what will be an almighty bust up.

The final day of the case begins with both the defendants James (or Cameron as he once was known), and Elizabeth, standing in the dock as the defence and prosecution lay out their final speeches.
The jury retires to consider all the evidence.

Three hours later, the jury come back in, and court is back in session as the remaining friends, other associates and gathered press take their seats.
Josh, Geoff, and Andrew talk amongst themselves, wondering what the verdicts will be for both James and Elizabeth, and how long they will get inside.
John, Tom, and Tyler sit with them, watching the other people filter in. the gathered press ready to record and report the outcomes of this high-profile case, which has made national news. All the major TV channels have reporters inside and outside too, ready to go live.

The Jury comes back and reads out their verdicts, with no surprises based on the evidence seen and heard.

James is found guilty of four murders, that of Enrique, Rebecca, Harry, and the other man called George. He is found guilty of plotting the murder of Sebastian. He is also found guilty of all other lesser offences that are related or unrelated to the series of events.
Elizabeth is found not guilty of murder but guilty of aiding and abetting a murderer and helping to conspire and deceive and pervert the course of justice, and the lesser mentioned crimes too.

Once the verdicts have been read out, the judge then hands down the sentences to both James and Elizabeth. James is given four life terms, with no chance of parole until at least forty years have been served, with psychiatric reports and evaluations to be administered on a regular basis to ascertain his mental capacity to even have a chance of being released ever again.
Elizabeth, surprisingly, gets quite a light sentence, because although she has been a major factor in this whole affair, she is not exactly caught telling her husband to kill those people, that the evidence isn't strong enough to convict her of plotting.
Instead, she is given four years prison time for perverting the course of justice and for helping her husband to conceal evidence of crimes committed.

As the verdicts are read out, and the judge gives his damning closing speech about the heinous crimes committed by James and helped by his scheming wife, they are led away separately to the waiting police vans outside, to be taken away to their respective prisons to begin their sentences.

Outside, the gathered press and national news channels are having a field day with the contents of the case, trying to film and interview anyone associated with the case. Even Josh and his friends are accosted by the press, as they are known to have been in the same circles as James and Elizabeth, especially being neighbour's. Nothing is insinuated against them, but the press wants their stories, something that Josh and the others act wisely to not give, as they make their way out of court and make their way to waiting taxis to whisk them away.

The friends head to Josh's home, where they are greeted by Judith, Claire, Katie, and Lynda. Outside Josh's home some of the national and local press have arrived, wanting to hear their story, but to no avail. Clio, Indya, Maddie, Nicole, and Kirsty are nowhere to be seen or heard from, nor are Steve, Phil, and Dominic. No surprises there then. "So, what now?" Andrew asks the group. "I think its fair to say that some of the others have a lot of talking to do" says Judith. "Let's leave them to it, let's not get involved, this is a mess as it is" replies Tyler, to which the friends nod along. Katie phone pings as she looks at it to see who has messaged, but also notices that all those that have bene involved in some way with Elizabeth and James, have left the group, leaving the others.

It has come as no surprise really. In the space of one year, two people have caused the breakup of what was once a tight knit group of friends, splitting loyalties down the line for some, but for the others they stay true to each other, able to at least hold their heads up high that they played no part in this Hitchin affair. Hitchin's self-proclaimed high society group has suddenly come tumbling down.

One Year Later:
Life Blows on

The reverend James is behind bars and, quite surprisingly, still preaches and acts as a man of the cloth, albeit one that has committed multiple sins. He has also started up a relationship with another inmate, well, with several men!. It seems his instincts don't stop just because he is locked up.

Elizabeth too is still behind bars, but is eligible for parole in another years' time, having demonstrated good behaviour. She too has struck up several relationships in her prison. Not that seems to come as a surprise.

Josh and Judith are still together, stronger than ever, having endured the past twelve months of being in the middle of the friendship group. Both continue with their lives and still live on Knights Road in Hitchin.
They remain close friends with Geoff and Claire, and with Katie and Andrew, and of course Tom and Tyler.

John and Lynda have gone quiet on the social scene and haven't been seen out much, nor do they make much contact with the others.

Tom and Tyler are now the proud parents of an adopted child, and they spend their free time raising their family, whilst maintaining their businesses.

Steve and Kirsty somehow managed to patch things up together, and although to the outside world they look like they are a strong couple, behind the scenes they are not good, with regular arguments. Kirsty only stayed with Steve because she wouldn't have anywhere to go if they did split up, and he earns well, so it is now more a coupling of convenience.
Andrew and Katie continue their hedonistic lifestyle with regular meetings with other couples and remain good friends with Josh, Judith, Goeff and Claire.

Geoff and Claire continue to build their business empires as they go from strength to strength, keeping their friendship group strong as ever.

Phil and Maddie have split up. He has moved out of their home, the house up for sale and divorce proceedings are under way. They were going to try and give it a go, but once Maddie gave birth to the baby, a quick DNA test revealed that James is the father of the child, and this is something that Phil couldn't live with. At present, Phil is living with Dominic in a rented flat.

Maddie is living in a flat that is owned by John and Lynda, who felt sorry for her, especially as she is with child. Maddie has lost her businesses and is now reliant on the lesser income of Phil plus any benefits she is entitled to from the state. Phil's business is struggling, trying to make ends meet once all financial outgoings have been paid out.

Dominic and Nicole have split up. Dominic still works at the hospital. Nicole has moved out of their home and into her own flat, as they wait for their divorce and house sale to go through. Nicole continues her work, but scandal has hit her business quite somewhat.

Indya continues to live where she does and has since remarried. She doesn't have much to do with anyone anymore, she has moved on it seems.

Clio lost her home. Harry's dodgy business dealings came home to roost with him no longer present. She has lost everything and currently lives with her parents. Clio has never had a career and cannot afford to buy her own place. Out of everyone, she has fallen the most, apart from James and Elizabeth of course!
One surprise does remain, and that is Clio and Elizabeth have kept in contact...

THE END... for now!

Acknowledgments:

Thank you to the businesses mentioned in this book that gave permission to use them so that the readers may see some familiarity with the locations. Some places of course have been made up, but for those that are not, thank you!

To David Wardle of Bold & Noble for another great front cover creation, as he did so with my first novel, War Olympus! As always, my good man, keep carrying that bag!

To Adam Rossington at Altitude Drone Surveys for your drone footage of the initial images to create the front cover!

To my front cover "dead" bodies that are: Raphaella Thompson, Steve Parry, Ben Fuller, Callum Hare, and Dan Robinson!

Thanks as always to my long-suffering family!

Thanks to the Burnt Hare Events Family for their humour and support, and to all my friends that encourage me!

Any names, other places, people or other, are purely fictional and any similarity apart from the above-mentioned businesses that gave permission and the town of Hitchin and some referenced roads and locations, everything else is purely coincidental and unintended.

You can follow the latest on my book releases via my social media page, as well as following my other pages on social media that are for sporting events in the town that I love, Hitchin!

Printed in Great Britain
by Amazon